Acclaim for Christian Kiefer's
One Day Soon Time Will Have No Place Left to Hide

"The best experimental American writing doesn't have to look funny on the page, as mainstream Irish story writer Frank O'Connor once defined experiment. It takes us down into the interstices of intelligence and shows us just what it is that connects everything, from the grand to the ridiculous, to everything else. Heartbreak in a line break, wisdom by means of punctuation. Christian Kiefer knows this, shows us, leads us in work such as this onward, ever onward, into new realms of experience. I'm now a dedicated follower."

—Alan Cheuse, author of *Prayers for the Living*

"In an exceptional novella as much about constructing narrative as it is about negating it, Christian Kiefer brilliantly breaks down the fourth wall to lure us into a world of walls: literal and metaphorical, physical and ethereal, those between people, those between spaces, those between times, and those ambiguous ones between art and life."

—Susan Steinberg, author of *Spectacle*

"In his cool mercury depiction of the life of a conceptual artist in the American West, Christian Kiefer's killer novella brings to mind, all at once: Joan Didion, Don DeLillo, William T. Vollmann, and even a sly heady whiff of Thomas Pynchon. But the heart that pounds in the chest of *One Day Soon Time Will Have No Place Left to Hide* reveals itself in the burdened, complicated relationship between Frank and Caitlin Poole. The metafiction in this novella will draw you in with its winking intellect, but the fully realized humans under its synthetic skin will keep you reading. Christian Kiefer is a masterful stylist with ideas to burn."

—Daniel Torday, author of *The Last Flight of Poxl West* and *The Sensualist*

"A truly cinematic novella. Wildly inventive. Harnesses the spirit of Don DeLillo and Mark Danielewski to create something utterly original and moving. You'll want to read it more than once."

—Nicholas Rombes, author of *The Absolution of Roberto Acestes Laing*

"Christian Kiefer's new novella-cum-documentary blueprint, *One Day Soon Time Will Have No Place Left to Hide*, makes public 'the privatopia beyond the noise wall...' and compels the bizarre to bump-and-grind with the quotidian, the world without with the world within, finding—via his delightfully unexpected characters (one of which may or may not be the reader-as-voyeur), and prose that marries the hilarious with the incantatory—that the best of our sad holinesses lurk beneath the asphalt of our parking lots, a cone emptied of its ice cream, and all agonizing estrangement that confuses itself for a nostalgia fetish. The result feels like a cockeyed and spot-on guided tour through our entire-lives-flashing-before-our-eyes, as entertaining as it is disquieting, as dreamy as it is terrestrial—and in Kiefer's universe, these reactions are deliciously indistinguishable from one another."

—Matthew Gavin Frank, author of *The Mad Feast* and *Preparing the Ghost*

ONE DAY SOON TIME WILL HAVE NO PLACE LEFT TO HIDE

CHRISTIAN KIEFER

NOUVELLA

2015

This is a work of fiction. Names, characters, places and incidents are either the product of the author's imagination or are used fictitiously, and any resemblance to actual persons, establishments, events or locales is entirely coincidental.

**ONE DAY SOON TIME WILL HAVE
NO PLACE LEFT TO HIDE**

Alan Cheuse
1940-2015

One Day Soon Time Will Have
No Place Left to Hide

Let us be clear.

The time you spend reading these words

will not be returned.

FADE IN:

THE WORLD WITHIN THE WORLD

His name is Frank Poole and he likes ice cream. The public park in which he sits with his wife, Caitlin, is otherwise empty. They slouch into the cold, these two, seated side-by-side at the edge of a concrete picnic table, each clutching a paper cup and scooping ice cream slowly into their mouths with tiny plastic spoons, pausing now and again to peer out at the green slope, the occasional lethargic car that passes on the road, the row of silent suburban homes facing the playground. A few hundred yards off, a flock of starlings bursts forth from a stand of stark black trees, forms a series of undulating shapes, and settles once more into those bare spindly branches. From this distance they make no sound whatsoever, their display part of the same pale wash that covers everything.

The two have settled into an identical silence and yet it is not an uneasy one. Frank looks slowly at the empty scene, not with affectation or import or meaning, but merely gazing at what is before him. Tufts of goose down bloom from the split lining of his jacket and the sock hat pulled over his tousled hair is equally battered and unraveling. As for Caitlin, at his side in that long quiet, she sits in similarly disheveled garb. Had you not already known them, you might imagine that they are homeless or at least downtrodden by economics or by circumstance, and yet none of these observations are true.

Caitlin is more frenetic than Poole, fifteen years his junior and lacking whatever deep center of gravity allows him to sit there on the edge of the table, unmoving, without expression or judgment. She pulls at her knit scarf, fidgets with the paper cup. But that is how they work together, these two. It is their balance. Ragged, thin as wisps, and bound to each other.

Silence everywhere on earth and the park the distal point around which it rotates.

When his voice comes, it is from one side of a recorded interview. We cannot hear the interviewer. Instead it is only Frank: halting, sometimes muffled as if by a hand, sometimes nearly inaudible.

Frank Poole. My name is Frank Poole.

Listen, before we go any further: Is this really how it's going to start? I mean, with the ice cream?

I don't know. It's your thing.

No, not weird. Just...I don't know...awkward or something. Anyway, go ahead.

No, no. It's your thing. You just do it. I shouldn't have said anything. You ask your questions.

No, not that. I don't want to talk about that. Ask me something else.

What I'm doing now?

Let's not call it "the development."

No, just call it what it is.

One Day Soon Time Will Have No Place Left to Hide. *Yeah,* One Day Soon Time Will Have No Place Left to Hide.

No, it's no place. Not nowhere.

It has to be no place. It's important.

Because it's no place. Not nowhere. Nowhere can be anything. No place is specific.

No, I'm not. I'm not upset about it. I'm just trying to tell you why it's no place and not nowhere.

He has been done with his ice cream for some time and he rises now and throws the empty cup into the wire trash bin and then stands, staring down into the container. After a moment he reaches inside. Caitlin says nothing. Both of them silent. A bird chirps cautiously in the sharp bright air.

Sometimes you might find something in here you can use, he says at last, to the camera or to Caitlin or to you.

Or eat, she says.

He chuckles. Yeah, that too. Here's a hamburger.

How much of a hamburger?

About half.

I'll give you a dollar if you eat that.

I don't want to eat that.

Two dollars then.

You're a riot, he says, deadpan. He pulls something out that he likes. A cardboard drink holder. That's interesting, he says.

Not really, Caitlin says. There is a glimmer of humor in her voice.

He continues to look at it, turning it over in his hands. No, he says at last. No, it's good.

Whatever you say, Frank, she says. She's ribbing him, gently.

I think I'd like some more ice cream, he says, still

4

staring at the cup holder in his hands.

Beyond them: a short rise. The grass freshly cut but also run through with stripes of mud. Were you to place your ear so close, you would hear running water as if a tide, a current, a rushing stream flowing over smooth stones to the sea.

Time to go, Frank.

Is it?

Yep. Stuff to do.

He turns to look at us, at you, his eyes across the grass, the rushing water, the sky, the paper, the words. OK, let's go, he says.

Buildings and landscapes without beauty. But is this not America? Here a parking lot. Here an unfinished meal resting on the table of some desert casino cafe. A factory set against a gray sky. Blank featureless walls. Empty living rooms with deer heads mounted on vinyl siding. Plastic ceiling lamps meant to look like clusters of grapes. Televisions that display no image but a singular square of black slate. Clouds scudding across empty space the color of concrete.

Then anonymous prefabricated homes. Modern ones. Midsized. One after another. All essentially the same. Perfect lawns. Clean windows. No one home. Nothing inside. Vacant. Again and again.

And finally four white faces. They stare back at you from their sofa. The parents. The children: a boy and a girl. The wallpaper behind them: It is a tangle of blue branches, blue leaves, blue birds.

We have come to understand the language. The way the cut implies movement across time, across physical space. We understand how it can be used to rotate around a point so that we can see one speaker and then reverse to reveal the response. His or hers. A strip of grass meant to remind us where we are, that there is a location and that we occupy it, at least for the moment. We have learned to be ready for the edit in the same way we have learned to look at a painting or a photograph, how we have come to understand what is meant to be real and what is not. The novelist's ellipsis. The poet's stanza break. The moves that keep us moving, that delay the fade and so delay the moment when the lights come up and one world disappears for another.

And so their home. The room we enter is a moment leaning toward a goal: stacked books and papers, notes and diagrams, architectural drawings and blueprints. It is amidst such materials that we find Frank Poole, a desk lamp jutting out from the stacks before him as if to indicate that somewhere, under all the material of his inquiry, might sit a desk or table of some kind. He leans into its yellow glow, his eyes in the open pages of a book, a pencil in one hand, its eraser tapping a notebook scribbled with words and lines and abstract doodles. Tap tap. Tap tap. The pages next to his hand contain a scrawled design not unlike a mandala or some intricate maze arranged in a circle, the center of which is itself a circle. But this we see only for a fleeting instant, for we do not linger, instead continuing to drift over the stacks without pause, the items that pass within our view a slow moving blur—notes in Poole's hand, crumpled architectural blueprints and sketches, a scattering of books on time and clock-making— and then we are across those stacks, moving, with purpose now, toward a second yellow light that spills out of the kitchen and dining room.

Caitlin stands at a wall calendar decorated with images from illuminated medieval manuscripts, a spatula in one hand and the telephone in the other, its spiral cord dangling nearly to the floor. The room beyond her is the opposite of the space from which we have come: tidy, scrubbed, organized, lit by sunlight that slants through a broad sliding glass door framing a bright, grassy backyard.

He's not giving interviews right now, she says into the phone.

I'm sorry, he's just not. Maybe once the project's done.

Yes, that's what it's called. *No Place*. That's right.

No, I can't comment on that.

Thank you. Bye now.

Frank's voice calls from the piled books and papers in the living room: They get the name right at least?

Yep.

The whole thing?

Yeah, the whole thing.

They keep saying "nowhere." That doesn't even make sense.

He said it right.

Reporters, Frank says.

She has turned to the stovetop again and shakes a sizzling pan, the sausages within turning and jumping. People want to know what's happening, she calls into the other room. That's good, right?

It's distracting.

I know it is. But it's good too. *The New York Times*.

It's still distracting no matter who it is.

From across the room, in the mote of illumination, Poole makes brief eye contact, as if to mark your presence, as if to mark that the gauze of text you now read is itself a disruption in the flow of his work. It is a glance so fleeting that when it is over you wonder if it has occurred at all.

You want me to pack for you? she calls to him.

Probably. Clothes anyway.

Tuesday's the day.

What's today? Friday?

Saturday.

OK.

You're gonna need to sort which books you want to bring.

OK on that too.

Did you want to look at lighting today or do you want to try to do that out there?

I'm not really thinking about that right now.

I'm just going to have to ask you again later.

He glances up from the table and for the briefest instant he meets your impassive gaze with a look of exhaustion and surrender. If Caitlin offers some similar expression from the sunlit glow of the kitchen, you do not see it, but her voice comes a moment later: Frank?

I heard you.

And now silence.

Frank returns to the books on the table but it is clear his attention is, for the moment, on something else: perhaps Caitlin in the kitchen, perhaps your presence, hovering in the room like a ghost. His eyes flit over the materials before him. Then he seems to shake himself clear of whatever aberrant thought has pulled him away. It is a kind of transformation from one state of being to another, his shape leaning forward, almost imperceptibly, toward the open page as profound stillness floods out over the frame.

For a long time there is only that stillness. A few tentative sounds from the kitchen. Frank's undeviating gaze.

The page displays a black and white photograph of a house with a smiling white family standing before it, their station wagon hitched to a boat, roof stacked high with luggage.

Mayonnaise, he says quietly.

It is hardly louder than a whisper and yet Caitlin's voice responds from the kitchen. What's that? she calls.

Lots of white people, he says, more loudly this time. Maybe I should paint all the houses black.

You're not going to do that.

No, you're probably right.

I am right but it would be great if you would.

Maybe I will then, he says. He pauses for a moment. Then he says, to himself: *The New York Times*. He says it as if it's a little song, a jingle. *The New York Times*.

Caitlin sets a plate in front of him. Sausage and

toast. Eat, she says, simply.

Eat eat, he says. He's in a kind of daze, his mind somewhere else, maybe inside the papers and books spread out before him on the table, with the family ready to leave on their vacation. Some other time. Some other where and when.

The New York Times and houses for white people, he mumbles.

Frank?

What?

We still need to talk, you know.

About what?

There is no verbal response at first but then she appears, standing in the kitchen doorway with the spatula still held in her hand, the other limp at her side, then creeping up to rest on her cocked hip, then dropping again. She glances at you only briefly, as if considering whether this conversation should be any of your concern. Frank? she says.

What?

We still need to talk about it.

We will.

So you say.

We will, Cait.

Promise?

Cross my heart, Poole says. He has not deviated

his gaze from the images in the books. The suburbs. Perfect houses. Perfect white families in perfectly similar ranch style homes, again and again.

Caitlin continues to hover in the doorway, not speaking, only watching him amidst the papers and photographs. Eat, Frank, she says into that silence.

OK, Poole says. We can no longer see him so we do not know if he begins eating or not. He has once again faded into the images and words, into the ideas sprawled all around him.

She is slow to turn away and when she does at last it is to move across the room to the antique desk that hugs the wall beside the sliding glass door. She rolls back the tambour and sits at the clean surface within, opening a leather-bound planner and flipping through various calendar pages until she reaches October 15. Beyond her, the backyard is fleeing into winter: muddy grass surrounded by aged gray fencing.

We're supposed to leave in three days but he's not going to be ready, Caitlin says over her shoulder, quietly, confidentially.

Are you talking about me? Frank calls from the other room.

Of course I am, she responds.

Don't tell any secrets.

Are there secrets?

There are always secrets.

The light that slants through the window is the color of fresh butter. A checked print countertop and wallpaper as from the early 1980s. The antique rolltop desk, its cubbies lined with orderly stacks of documents. The sink white and the faucet handle designed like a well pump. A house in the Midwest but apart from the well pump faucet it might exist anywhere at all.

He won't be ready, she says to us, to you. She smiles briefly, shrugs. Abandon all hope ye who try to get Frank Poole anywhere on time.

I'll be ready, he calls from the front room.

All lies, she says in response. Nothing but lies, lies, and more lies.

[4]

The television images are copied and recopied from aged videotape so that what we see is filled with video distortion. The Museum of Natural History and Science in Cincinnati. We can still hear their home life, although Frank and Caitlin are quiet now and we are left with the sounds of the house itself, of the rooms in which they are looking through their various papers. Their pens and pencils scratching. The sound of yellow sunlight and the map of America upon which they live.

On the screen, Frank Poole is much younger than the man we have already seen, perhaps in his early twenties, smiling shyly as a series of reporters ask him questions we cannot hear. Now a diorama from a museum. A cave man standing over the antler rack of a dead elk. And then Frank again, smiling sheepishly, gazing with an expression of vague bemusement at the reporters and the cameras.

An Iroquois woman breastfeeds beside a field of corn.

A grizzly stands to look out through the glass.

It is on a chill Wednesday four days later that they finally drive away, their white Mercury swinging clear of the quaint Midwestern court in which their home and two others face a broad semi-circle lined with cracked asphalt and browning flowers. A neighbor waves, her pink bathrobe pulled up around her throat. Good luck, she calls to the car. Frank waves through the closed window, his face showing no emotion at all, his mouth moving as if in mid-sentence. Caitlin behind the wheel. The backseat and roof rack piled high with boxes and the car rocking slowly as it ambles down the short house-lined drive and onto the main road beyond.

The neighbor stands in the vacancy. Her hair is an unnatural color of red, almost maroon. Those two? she says. Sweet as pie. Really. You couldn't ask for any better neighbors. I guess he's a big time artist or something. Probably works at the university. And Caity's just the sweetest girl. Like how you'd want your daughter to be, you know?

She continues to smile, staring out at where the court empties into the road beyond, her breath a swirl of steam rising into the gray air.

I told her she'll be a good mother. I really did. I thought she was gonna cry when I said that. Thirty's not so old to have a baby anyway. Not these days.

The smile frozen upon her face is almost a grimace.

Just exactly like apple pie, she says.

And the white Mercury, it is already long gone.

SIX DIFFERENT
STYLES

[1]

The photographs are mostly black and white, clipped from magazines and books, some badly photocopied from unknown sources, copied and recopied so that what remains is a spattering of dark patches that are difficult to bring into any sense of shape or meaning. Most of the images are scrawled with notes and arrows and unreadable words. When they shift position, it is, at first, as if they have moved under their own power. Then his hand crosses the frame, only for a moment, sliding one image away and tilting another into position. As if in explanation. As if such a thing as a photograph could explain everything to come after.

1961. The photograph—this photograph—is familiar. The boat on its trailer. Before it, in the center of the frame, the station wagon with its roof stacked with luggage. And then the four of them in the foreground, positioned uncomfortably as if ready, at any moment, to flee.

The voice we hear is Frank's:

> *I just want it to be something beautiful. You know? Like something with a point. Yeah, well, I know that. I know I did that but look it's like you can't just go back to what it was. You know? Those things are specific.*
>
> *The convenience store. The McDonald's inside that guy's apartment.*
>
> *I mean, I'm proud of that stuff but it has its form and its function. Specific purposes. You know?*

They are typical, we presume. The man wears sunglasses and a mustache and stares into the lens with a look of ownership. And perhaps such a look says all that need be said. Everything within the frame is mine and mine alone. A thumb hooked into his pocket. The woman wraps an arm around her daughter. Their next oldest, a towheaded boy in a white t-shirt—perhaps ten or eleven years old—stands nearest the front of the car while their youngest, also a boy and also towheaded, kneels at their feet, clutching the family dog.

The house behind them has no identifiable features at all: a small ranch house not unlike the Pooles' Iowa home. A hedge. A lawn so flat and gray that it might be concrete. All of this is owned in the way we own anything of such personal magnitude: bought on credit and paid in installments. The daughter will have three children of her own by the time the last house payment is made. And of the two towheaded boys: one will spend his life selling cars to one day retire into a house not unlike this one; the other will die at the edge of a rice paddy in a country not one of them has yet heard of. It is not a sad story. It is only the story that is.

[3]

Roseville, Minnesota, circa 1955. Bicycles and children.

> *I mean, it's not just the houses and the land-scapes but the people. They're looking back at you and you have to know that they're all old or a lot of them are dead or whatever. But in the photographs it's like time's frozen. You know? Like someone put it in a bottle or something. Bottled it.*
>
> *Yeah, well, you keep bringing those projects up and I get it but this isn't that. Those are specific kinds of arrest. Arresting physical space. This is space and time, intertwined in a way. You know? I mean deeply wrapped together like the strands in a rope. Like a double helix or something.*

The little girl looks sadly away from the camera, to something outside the frame of the lens. Checkerboard pants and low white socks. The other girls are posing with their bicycles but this girl, this sad girl, has no such mode of transportation. Beyond them: a faint slow hill. A handful of homes not unlike the rows of mailboxes that run across the middle distance.

Six years after this photograph, the sad girl will sneak off to the movies with a boy two years older than she is. The boy has a car of his own, a well-used Pontiac Safari station wagon, and she thinks the car, the fact that he has a car, to be a wonderful thing. The night of the movies is their first date but not their last. Later, she will tell her children that the night of the movies was the single most important night of her life.

There are some stories that are not simply tales of woe.

4

And then we come to Levittown, Pennsylvania. The year is 1957. Histories of the development of suburbia will point to Levittown as the prototype for all to come after. Such books will characterize the diaspora from urban centers as "the white flight," an apropos and essentially correct designator for the ethnic fears that lay, in 1957, in clear view for anyone willing to look.

Here they are: gray rectangles broken into quadrants. The sloping gray roofs. The slate gray lawns. A sky broken only by the pale curve of artistically rendered clouds. There is nothing any of us could use to differentiate one from another. We would forget them the moment our eyes turned away but that does not mean they are empty. Indeed, our forgetfulness is why he holds such an idea in his mind. Because they are the same. Because they are comprised of flat plates of perfect colorless space. Because you do not know how to look at such a thing at all.

> *What you want is something you can't reach.*
> *I mean that's the idea, right? It's like an endless*
> *closed loop. But that's like your DNA really or*
> *something like that. I mean, look, it's the stuff*
> *that makes you who you are, on a basic basic*
> *level, but it's not like you can load it into your*

computer and see what it is. That's what I mean.
It'll be just closed up at the end.

No, never. But we'll have video feeds. Like you
could look it all up on the internet or whatever.
We're going to have close to a hundred angles
inside so you'll be able to see what it looks like
just like you were inside but that's the thing,
right? You won't be inside. No one will be. Ever.

Look it's not entertainment, you know? It's
something else. It ain't will be set up for maxi-
mum entertainment value and economics. I
mean not everything can be like that. Some
things have to be left outside.

This is about creating a moment that doesn't
end. You know?

I mean, hell, that's why it's called what it's called.

One of four different styles of the Jubilee. One of
five different styles of the Pennsylvanian. One of four
different styles of the Country Clubber. One of four
different styles of the Levittowner. A flyer that comes
tumbling out of a book. See how it unfolds in the air.
Its spiral path to the carpet. No figures present in the
images at all and even if there were they too would be
caught in that bubble of time. Within those flat planes
in empty space. Clean and perfect and colorless.

Unknown interior, circa 1950s. Oh their hollow-eyed stare. Like religious fanatics. Like car salesmen. Like self-help authors. Perhaps like you.

> *Yeah, I guess there's a social function too.*
> *I mean, look, these are literally cookie cutter.*
> *I mean, it's what the term comes from.*
> *Sameness, right? Even in the names. Jubilee?*
> *Pennsylvanian? Country Clubber? I mean, come*
> *on, right? It's like a put on. But it's not a put on.*
> *Not really. It's something else.*
>
> *No, it's not nostalgia. I don't believe in nostalgia. It's time. You know? I mean right now time.*
> *Today. That kind of clock. That kind of now.*

They sit arranged on the sofa in an attitude of having been both posed and unposed. She holds open the paper—the *Herald Tribune*—but her eyes are on you. Her husband to the side in his three-piece suit, looking like an ad executive. And the children—it is impossible to decide who is the older, perhaps they are twins—are arranged behind their parents. She sits on the arm of the sofa, something her parents would never have allowed were it not for this moment, for the moment of the photograph.

And who is to say any of them are related at all? Pin them to the bird-branch wallpaper. To the *Herald Tribune*. To the white padded sofa. Pale wallpaper. Pale faces staring back at you.

A false family of models but their lives will play out along the only lines that exist. Time a ratchet turning forward all the gears.

Except this one.

41st PARALLEL NORTH

[1]

A parking lot by a small gas station beyond which sprawl fast food restaurants and more gas stations, sometimes intermingled, sometimes separated by medians in which tattered dwarf trees stand like empty symbols pointing out some semiology of absence. Farther out, at the edge of the buildings and lights and signs and rushing cars, the landscape stretches away as a flat plain cut by occasional patches of irrigated farm fields. Shades of green arrayed in rows.

He scribbles notes on what subject we do not know and then stands clicking the Polaroid. That familiar unscrolling of undeveloped film.

Eisenhower, he says.

Ike, Caitlin says.

I like Ike, he says.

Yeah, me too. Are we gonna eat here?

Next one.

OK.

Unless you're super hungry. I'm not really hungry yet.

I'm not hungry enough to eat here.

All right.

She is restless but then she always is. It is simply impossible for her to stand still the way Frank does, staring out into the distance as if there is something of interest there but when she looks it is only the end of the earth and the beginning of the sky, the same as it has ever been, and she sees no reason to stare. She hops up to sit on the hood of the car, then hops down again. You about ready to hit the road? she asks.

I was trying to remember…isn't there a Lincoln statue or something on the way? Is that in this state?

Wyoming.

Is that where it is?

Yeah, somewhere. We stopped there last time we drove 80. It was snowing. She tucks her scarf up around her neck.

Yeah, that's right, he says. It's like a giant head or something. By the freeway. A pause and then he adds, We need like a roadside attraction guidebook.

We're missing all the giant balls of twine.

Alligator wrestling.

Wrasslin', she says.

Yeah, wrasslin', he says. Gator wrasslin'. He scratches his head through the sock hat and then says, Ike makes the road but Abe gets the giant head.

That's how it works, she says.

Yep, he says. That's right. Maybe there's gator wrasslin' somewhere along the way.

I doubt it, she says.

So do I but you never know. Wyoming is coming up, right?

Couple hours. Then Utah and then Nevada.

Here comes Honest Abe.

Let's go, Frank.

All right.

Your turn to drive.

Crap.

Maybe, but still your turn.

All right, he says.

She hands him the keys.

From the air there is a sense of beauty. The landscape unfurling in all directions like a maze of interlocking shapes, the fractal depth of which is breathtaking in its ingenuity. Cul-de-sacs feather into themselves. Gray roads split into streets and courts and boulevards. There is the box-like similarity of roof after roof after roof. And the occasional brilliant blue rectangle of a pool like a precious gem set amongst the complexity of line and shape like the details of a Tibetan sand painting. Everything clean and directed and possessed of an intelligence which is the intelligence of order set forth in the hearts of men and beasts, in the intellect of a fiddlehead, in the soul of the waters that make up what we are.

I will give you the names, not because they supply the landscape with meaning but because they do not. Cluster and glut. Landfill and greenfield. Duck and TOAD and strip. And here: the wrought iron gate of the privatopia. Beyond the noise wall, the rush of freeway traffic continues unabated. Cover your ears and the hiss and hum comes yet through the curvature of your skull.

Caitlin's words, her voice, scrolling over that same landscape. Over the edge nodes and car parks. Over

the ozoners and LULUs. Over the snout houses in
their gently curving rows.

Sure. Sure.

*It's all about time, really. I mean it's obvious,
isn't it?*

*Yeah, but maybe you should ask Frank about
that.*

*Yeah, OK. I get that. He's not the most
explanatory guy. Look, his head is in the work
all the time. I mean really in the work. You can't
have an ice cream cone with him and not have
something come up. So that's something you just
have to accept and kind of go with.*

*So, yeah, I guess. I mean but you have to
understand that this is my take on the project.
Not his.*

*So everything he's done has been really circling
the idea of time itself as a physical force. Right?*

*The new project is an extension of the kind
of stuff he's done before. Thematically. Even
materially. But of course this is bigger and
more complete. He's been talking about how
this might just be it, you know? Like the whole
thing. Because what could he do afterward?
He'd have to do something totally different,*

because this pretty much has every possible aspect to it, all at once. I mean, look, it's a whole suburb, right? And then it will be sealed off.

It's finding a way to stay unchanged. In total. In time. Sometimes he calls it a snowglobe. That's pretty much it, right? Like a snowglobe. Of this particular moment in time. It's like America under glass.

He'd probably hate everything I just said. I mean, really, he'd rather people not talk about it like this. Well, me maybe.

No, I mean I'm probably the one who shouldn't talk about it. Because there's going to be a sense that I'm an expert or something.

Me? No way. I'm no more expert than you are. Frank would tell you he's not the expert either. You are. You and me and everyone. That's the point. Or a point. But now I'm explaining it again instead of shutting my trap like I should be.

Everything designated by zone. Single detached residential. Low density infill. Residential small lot. And then shopping centers and low intensity business and commercial mixed. Parking lots for budget hotels. Then gas stations, fast food restaurants, manufactured housing aligned in rows the color of dirt. McDonald's, from the sky, just the same as on the ground: a circus tent belching dark smoke into the concrete air. The zone of the highway corridor.

Seventeen-hundred-miles across that landscape in a line very nearly due west. 41st parallel north. The route of pioneers. Of Greeley's young American men bent on self-improvement. Of dreamers and vagabonds and fools. All interstate freeways run through such landscapes as these. Endless arteries flowing in all possible directions. Some of them reach from Iowa City to Winnemucca and Golconda and on toward Eden Valley. And at least one of them reaches to you.

[3]

Have you thought about what I said?

What you said when?

You know.

Oh. Yeah, I've thought about it a bit.

And?

And what?

I'm kinda freaking out here, Frank.

I don't want you to freak out.

So?

So what do you want me to say?

Frank, she says, exhaling through the wind, you're going to have to give me more than that. This isn't like making a project.

Well, it's sort of like making a project, he says.

No.

No?

No.

He shrugs.

You can't just stand there, Frank. That's not gonna work this time.

Does it ever work?

No, she says. There is a thin harsh quality to her words.

Around them, the landscape is flat and endless. More than a thousand miles yet to go. A thousand miles of nearly featureless landscape. That people have chosen this for their lives is something she simply cannot understand. You're gonna be a dad, she says.

I'm aware of that.

Are you ready?

Are you?

No, she says.

He looks at her now. You're not? he says.

Of course I'm not. She continues to stare out into the distance somewhere.

I didn't know that, he says.

Why do you think I want to talk about it?

I don't know why, he says. I thought you just wanted to talk about it. You talk. You know. About things.

That's what people do, Frank.

He shifts his gaze back to the distance, so that they are both staring out into the flat empty plain of America. The stillness enters him again. He does not move, does not even shift his weight. He may be thinking about parenthood or about the Eisenhower presidency or Abraham Lincoln or something else entirely.

You need to get your head around it, she says. I mean we both do.

I will. I am.

Are you?

Yeah, I am. I just have to get this project done first.

Her eyes flash up to his face. It is only for a moment before she looks away.

Their drift is into a space of silence, the two of them and the whole of America. 41st parallel north. His hand reaches for her, a gesture almost without thought. She takes it, neither of them looking at the other but connected, their fingers interlacing like the joined hands of teenagers.

It doesn't really work like that, she says at last.

Yes it does, he says. Yes it does.

[4]

And then pastures and orchards and neighbor-
hoods bumping against one another in abrupt and
swirling lines. The circles of irrigated green fields
and of black cul-de-sacs. Houses. Emptiness. Then
another rounded curl of box houses leapfrogging
across the fields like the tiny new fronds in the
crozier of a fern.

Caitlin behind the wheel. Frank beside her,
periodically snapping a photograph with his
Polaroid. The whirr of the film ejecting. He sits
waving it in the air in front of him. Light spins
through the car. Her eyes on the road, unmoving, watching the land come at her, come at them
both. There is nothing out there but the road
and emptiness. Boxes and bags and loose clothes
behind them, stacked to the roof of the car.

This is beautiful country, he says.

But it is not beautiful country. Flat dirt and
occasional farms. Her eyes. Her thin, closed mouth.
Caitlin in profile as farm country whips by the
window. Hair curling slowly in the wind. How it
circles and circles her face through Nebraska and
Wyoming. Through Utah. How it circles as they
drive into Nevada at last.

WHITE FISH

[1]

Water in the living room. Water in the kitchen.

They do not swim. They sit in recliners and on sofas. A man and a woman. A child. They are bathed in television light.

A slow white fish. A pale hand in the water.

Their voices: they too are under the surface. Hers first. And then his.

> *Frank?*
> *Yeah.*
> *You done with your ice cream?*
> *I'm done.*

You are surprised only at the immensity of the wall, even though you have known the general size of the project all along. But here it is, in physical reality, along the 41st parallel north, just past where that long channel westward crosses the 116th meridian: a steel wall that rises in a slow three-quarter circle, the diameter a full mile across, appearing—at a distance as you move up the temporary roadbed—like a thin gray stripe set against the desert, the mountains, the scattered cows, the endless sagebrush. But it grows as you approach, grows so slowly that you come to understand that your first view of it had been many miles distant, a view not from the freeway or indeed from any paved road at all, but only a good half-hour up the rocky dirt path that has been graded only as a temporary method of getting people and supplies and equipment to the project site. It is not much of a road at all and indeed you know that part of this particular project will be to eradicate this roadbed, to make sure that there is no clear way to get to the site. It will be empty space again. Mountains and cows and sagebrush.

The wall is open where it faces your approach, a gap of a hundred yards or more allowing for tractors and trucks to move into and out of the building site.

In the distance, the edges of the roof extend inside over the lip of that wall, leaning toward the outermost of the hundreds of steel pillars that jut up out of the crusty soil, pillars which stand now like guard towers, those in the center nearly one hundred feet tall, ready to support a roof system which has not yet been installed.

They walk together in this flat, walled plain, following the contractor's gestures as he points to the blueprint and then to the packed earth around them. It is colder here than it was in Iowa and their three streams of breath are visible as white smoke in the air.

So this is five thirty here, the contractor says, gesturing to a bare patch of dirt raked flat and from which juts a series of white pipes with protruding wires.

Frank stops and looks, first to the flat dirt and then to the contractor, who shows him the blueprint and points with a rough, stubby finger. Right here, the contractor says.

Five thirty p.m., Frank says.

PM, the contractor says, nodding.

I know it's right, Frank says.

The contractor looks at him but says nothing. Behind him, before him, on all sides: flat earth cut by roadbeds, each curved and curving toward a center, like a labyrinth, the steel supports jutting up everywhere like quills. The inside of the enclosing wall will be painted sky blue at some point but right now it is bare gray steel shining in the cold winter light.

I thought we were gonna have most of the foundations done by now, Frank says.

Yeah, that thing with the permits slowed us down some but we're trying to catch up.

How far behind are we? Caitlin says.

About a week, all told.

Frank nods.

Anyway, permit stuff is done now so we're plugging on. Should have this strip—he points to the map—five through maybe six and a half poured tomorrow.

Five through six thirty, Frank says.

Right, six thirty, the contractor says. He smiles as if it might be some kind of joke but Frank does not return the expression.

The forms are mostly done, the contractor says.

What about the truss system?

Later this week if all goes well.

They have come to a crossroads, dirt on all sides. The contractor points out site six. Frank would have called it six o'clock p.m., but he does not correct the contractor now. Nor does Caitlin. Instead, they both stand, watching, thinking about the days and nights to come, the dirt spreading out to that distant wall. Through the gap: the mountain ridge, a few miles beyond which runs the interstate, the same highway they took all the way from Iowa, pushing a long straight line across the map. We can hear its quiet hum even now. Like a breath. Like winter close on your heels.

[3]

The man jerks, breaks into pieces, echoes into himself, comes back together again. The film scratched and leaping off the sprockets, clacking and breaking apart and reconstituting once more. The man is laughing, silently. The man is coming to pieces. The man is laughing again.

A scattering of black scratches.

A coalescence of white white light.

[4]

The bathroom door is closed, its shape an outlined rectangle against the darkness.

Frank sits propped up on the bed. The television with its endless words and images. The sterility of the hotel room simply an indication of just how non-sterile it actually is.

Eden Valley, he says. Then he clears his throat and says it more firmly. Eden Valley. Well, almost to Eden Valley, anyway. In Nevada. When he shifts his weight, the bed makes the sound of crinkling plastic.

Well, the reality of making a large-scale project like this is that it has to be out in the desert some-where or you just can't afford it. I mean even out here, we wouldn't have been able to do it without a big chunk of land from the mining company and from the state of Nevada. Without that we'd have too much money in the property and not enough for the actual project. But really you'd need to talk to Cait about that stuff. She's in charge of all the money. I can't really deal with it.

His eyes do not deviate from the television. What gaze exists is weary, tired, blasted by the blue light of the screen.

Anyway, out here you can really get behind the idea of inaccessibility, you know?

His hand rises to stir the air and then returns to his lap once more.

That kind of perfection. Like Everest or something. Right. It's perfect, and then Tenzing and Hilary get to the top and now it's like an absurd Disneyland carnival up there. Crazy yellow oxygen tanks and people paying to go up there like it's a vacation. But why go there at all now? It's been used up so it's no longer a place in the way it was before. It's just not real anymore. I mean if you could eliminate all access to a place like that…

He trails off, shifts on the bed again. That crinkling. An undersheet perhaps. Or the blankets themselves, so freighted with nylon strands that they have become as if a plastic loaf. The voice on the television talks about cars. Then elephants. Then mutual funds. Then food.

Like a snow globe. She said that earlier? Good. That's perfect. Because that way it can be stopped. Flat.

He claps his hands together, as if to solidify the concept.

You take a museum diorama—something like Carl Akeley's or something…cavemen and huge vistas—and when you put it behind glass like they do there's no way to get to it anymore. But that's just an illusion too because there are ways for museum workers to get in or whatever, right? I mean one of my college jobs was dusting those things at the Field Museum, climbing in there after hours and getting it all spruced up again. That'll get you thinking.

Nothing is actually sealed off. But what this project does is really seal it off in a significant and permanent way. The whole thing. Like hermetically sealed. Time is, I mean.

The bathroom door opens. In the brightly lit space beyond, Caitlin stands at the mirror in profile, brushing her teeth in a t-shirt with a towel wrapped around her waist. She spits into the sink and rinses her mouth and spits again. When she is finished, she steps out of the bathroom, flipping the light off behind her and sliding under the sheet next to Frank, the towel remaining in a pool on the carpeted floor. What's on? she says.

Nothing. You wanna try?

He hands her the remote and she leans back and begins flipping through the stations. The elephants again. The cars. The mutual funds.

They sit like that for a long time, watching pieces of shows, Frank commenting now and then on an image. The fast food restaurant's logo. The used car dealer's suit. A slogan.

When the phone rings Frank lifts it from the nightstand and hands it across to Caitlin who answers without even glancing at him. Frank Poole's office, she says.

He glances at her now and she winks at him.

Oh hi, Mom, she says. She looks at you for a moment and then says, Hang on, and pulls the receiver away from her face. I'm gonna take this in the bathroom, she says.

All righty, Frank says.

She leans over him to grasp the base of the phone and then pulls it, its cord dragging out behind it across the room toward the bathroom door, her pale legs shining for a moment in the blue light of the television and then gone as the door swings closed behind her.

He is silent there on the bed for a time, watching the last channel she selected and then lifting the remote at last and clicking through to something else. The elephants change to a glassy mansion atop a cliff.

She's like the glue, he says. She's the one holding it all together.

He pauses, staring at the screen.

I met her when I was doing *For a Short Time Only*. That was after Cincinnati. She was part of the kids who were working on the project with me. That museum thing had hit pretty good but that didn't mean there was any money so I went down to the local high school and talked to their principal about having some of the kids come and help me put this project together. The museum things were really contained but the project I had in mind—the thing that turned into *For a Short Time Only*—wasn't really something I could do by myself and I didn't really have the money to hire out.

Yeah, well, she was seventeen. If you know what I mean. (He smiles at this little joke, this song within his words.) I was probably like thirty or something. Well, yeah, it wasn't like I swooped in like some weird old man or anything but there was a kind of, you know, arc there between us, right from go.

Well, yeah, she's the glue that keeps it running. That's a mixed metaphor but there you have it.

He continues to stare into the middle distance of the television.

Her voice is a murmur beyond the bathroom door and you are drawn to that faint susurration, to the white rectangle the door cuts into the dark air of the room. And her voice comes to you now, comes as if she is speaking into your ear, as if there is no door, as if she stands before you in her t-shirt, talking to her mother on the telephone in a hotel bathroom in a hotel casino in Winnemucca, Nevada. As if all of this is true.

Yeah, we just got here today. We went out there earlier and met with the contractor. It's coming. It's going to be a ton of work but it's coming, for sure. I'll send you some pictures.

I don't know.

Yeah, I guess.

No, we haven't really had a chance to talk much about that. Yeah, he's excited. Sure. Well, not that he's said but I know he is. Because I can tell, Mom. Can't you tell when Dad's excited about something? Well, I can tell with Frank anyway.

Look, I've got another call. I'd better take it. I love you too.

Frank Poole's office.

No, Frank's not giving interviews right now. I'm sorry but he's just not.

[5]

The television channels.

Somewhere Frank is in the water. Out of the shadows. Black mold on soaked plaster. His eyes closed and face pale. Hands of death. His hair adrift. Then into the shadow again. Out of focus. Lost.

You could change the channel and there would be elephants. And cars. And mutual funds. And there would be Frank with the white fish and the pale hands. Swimming and swimming though that dark water.

LUCKY

Let the names roll off your tongue: the Tuscarora
Mountains, the Sheep Creek Range, Boulder Valley,
the Shoshone Range, Antler Peak, the Cortez
Mountains, Buffalo Valley, Soldier Cap, Hot Springs
Peak, Eden Valley. Deserts and dirt and sagebrush.
An occasional cluster of cows standing motionless
on the scant dry plain.

Winnemucca, Nevada is part of this same
landscape: a scattering of houses and steel-roofed
buildings and fast food restaurants flung upon a
flat tableland between the high treeless mountains
of the Santa Rosa Range and the Sonoma. It is a
place perpetually howling with wind, the force of
which sweeps down through the passes and across
the yellow-tipped sagebrush that manages to hold, at

the base of each plant, a small hillock of black dirt. Indeed it sometimes feels as if the whole town might simply blow off the slopes and tumble end-over-end eastward, down Golconda Summit and into the flat sagebrush plain below, but of course it does not do so, instead clinging forever to the flanks of those low worn, bare peaks. A place for travelers to stop and refuel and for those in the outlying towns to the east and west to shop for food and clothing. Those who live here have lives not unlike those in any small American town. The industries are cattle ranching and open-pit mining and were it not for the bare scraggly earth both industries demand it is unlikely that Frank and Caitlin Poole would be here at all.

The main road through town is West Winnemucca Boulevard and it is here that we find the Lucky Hotel Casino, its name stacked one letter upon the next, below which runs backlit panels of signs indicating the wonders held within: Coffee Shop, Casino, Fun, Food, Cocktails. The glass doors are diagonal to the parking lot and as you pass through them you are struck immediately by the thick acrid scent of cigarette smoke and the various electronic bleeps and warblings from the slot machines that dominate the floor.

It is not a huge casino—not by the standards of

Las Vegas or even of Reno—but it is the largest in town. Digital screens are everywhere, animated with rolling numbers and letters and characters that pour past you as you move down the aisles. The signage above the far wall reads Pete's Coffee Shop, and you move toward that wall as if those letters mark a beacon of some kind. A sanctuary.

They sit within, at a small round-cornered table near the center of the room, the cigarette smoke from the casino floor drifting amongst the booths and scattered tables where anonymous diners perch like scraggly, bleary-eyed crows. Some of them glance toward you as you read these words. Some eyes hollow. Some shining. A man in a plaid shirt waves and his wife turns to stare at you. She continues to stare for a long, long time.

Frank eats a chicken fried steak with two runny and yet partially burned eggs floating at the edge of the plate. For Caitlin, it is two eggs scrambled, wheat toast in a small stack, a jumble of hash browns. They look up at each other periodically as they eat, their glances meeting above the condiment cage, above the jams and jellies, the Tabasco, the ketchup bottle.

He cuts his meat. Forks another bite into his mouth. How's your breakfast? he asks.

It's OK.

I like this place.

I know you do.

It's fun. It's like all of America in one place.

As if in response, the sound of jingling slot machines blooms through the door as it swings opens and then shrinks back to silence again.

I don't like being this close to the bar, she says.

I'm not worried about that.

I am.

Well, you don't need to be.

The couple at the table behind them has risen and staggers off toward the glass front of the building where the doors swing open upon the November street.

You don't worry about that? she asks him.

I don't think about it.

At all?

Well, not usually. He takes another bite. Chews. Swallows. I wish there was an ice cream place here, he says. I mean a good one. Even like 31 Flavors or something.

Bobtail.

Jeez, don't even say that, he says. That's just breaking my heart.

She takes a sip of her coffee and then says, So I

made an appointment for an ultrasound.

Is there something wrong?

No, it's just something you're supposed to do. I probably should have done one already.

He nods. He is not looking at her now. Instead he extracts a slice of wheat toast from the stack beside her plate and stirs it through his egg yolks.

So it's gonna be on Thursday. The doctor says we'll be able to see it. Maybe even if it's a boy or a girl.

Jeez, it's weird that they can tell.

Yeah, she says. So you should come too.

Oh, he says, clearly surprised. Can I?

Yeah, you can come to all this stuff. You're supposed to, even.

Oh, he says. OK, yeah.

Good, she says. She smiles at him. That's good. I'd really like that. And the doctor could answer any questions you had. You know. If you had any.

I don't even know where to start.

Good then, she says. You'll come.

The chicken fried steak is in pieces. I said I would, he says.

So um…there's something else we need to talk about.

He does not look up from his plate.

I talked to Mike today and we're already running pretty close on the budget.

How close? he says, his voice muffled through the mouthful of food.

Close, she says.

How close?

Really close, Frank.

He looks up at her now, his eyebrows arched in surprise. Maybe the NEH will kick down something, he says.

The deadline for that stuff is way past, she says.

His eyes are on his plate again, his fork tines through the yolk of his egg.

Look, she says, I think you're going to need to call the foundation.

And tell them what?

Tell them that you're gonna need fifty more to make sure the project gets done.

Fifty?

Maybe even—maybe like seventy-five. Just to make sure.

He does not respond, only sits fiddling with his fork.

Just to make sure, she repeats.

Jesus, he says now.

We don't really have a choice, Frank.

It's your job to deal with this stuff, he says. He does not look at her. He does not look at anything.

They won't listen to me at the foundation office. You know that.

Don't put this on me, he says. His voice is the same quiet deadpan and yet there is a faint charge of electricity in the phrasing.

What does that mean?

I make the art. You do the budget. That's what we do. He stirs at his egg as she stares at him. Shit, he says at last, I hate talking to those people.

Those people are making this whole thing possible, Frank.

I still hate talking to them.

Sometimes you need to step up.

I need to step up? He looks at her.

You might expect her to quail under the sudden intensity of his gaze but she does not, staring back at him, unblinking. You need to step up, Frank, she says, enunciating each clipped syllable.

He holds her gaze for a beat, two, and then nods. You're the boss, he says.

Goddamn right I am.

He returns to his plate; she continues watching him for a long moment before returning to her own.

The slot machine sounds filter in from the casino

floor. Video game bleeps and warbles. When she looks up at him again, she sees him staring at his plate, the fork gripped in his hand like a weapon.

Eat your breakfast, she tells him. It's gonna get cold.

It already is.

Well, it'll get colder then.

I doubt it, he says. He does not move.

[2]

The television images are copied and recopied from aged videotape so that what we see is filled with video distortion. The Museum of Natural History and Science in Cincinnati. The commentator introduces Frank Poole. And here he is. So much younger. Perhaps in his early twenties and smiling shyly as a series of reporters ask him questions about his work. The commentary is in official tones and it speaks of dioramas. Carl Akeley's work for the Museum of National History in New York. Frederick Blaschke's at the Field Museum in Chicago. But this is not New York or Chicago. This is Cincinnati and this is Frank Poole.

Then we see the work itself. Suburban scenes behind glass, not unlike those famous museum dioramas but also so very different. We are, of course, reminded of Blaschke's cavemen. The Azilian hunters readying their spears for the approaching boar. The Aurignacian painter blowing a haze of red to outline the shape of his hand on the wall of a cave. The Neanderthal family with its thickly muscled patriarch standing over the head and antlers of the elk he has killed while his mate and children sit within the shelter of the cave. But in place of the faux-taxidermied examples of primitive man are, instead, suburban figures in suburban homes. The cavemen of our memory are at least three-quarters facing the viewer, but these figures—Poole's figures—are all facing away. We stare at the back of a t-shirted man, his suit coat and shirt slung upon the bed, his slacks sagging across his ass. Across from him, the bathroom door is open and the light from within that space is blinding, as if we are looking directly into the sun. And there are others too, other windows, other glass-fronted interiors. A kitchen with a table set with plates of food and all the seated figures facing away, even the woman who sits at the head of the table. At the far end of that room, in the direction they are facing, the oven emits the same blinding light. And then another: this a living room where the figures face a television that in turn faces us, the light, perhaps predictably now, blasting out through the curved glass directly into our eyes.

The room where the audience mingles, slowly and in near silence, is awash in the shadows of the figures, the light from each enclosure cutting their dark forms from the empty space between them so that the viewers, as they wander from exhibit to exhibit, are enshrouded in their dark shapes, material then to the images held within, material to their opposites.

Who is to say that this television is any different from the television of the blinding light? Both televisions tell the same story. That he completed a project called *For a Short Time Only* and another called *Bottle Clock*. First gallery owners and art magazines take notice. Then the mainstream media: *Time* and *Newsweek* and *People*. In all cases, Frank finds the words they write about him, about his work, to be pretentious and embarrassing and absurd, even though he is in some ways pleased by the attention, pleased that he is no longer simply working in a vacuum of silence.

And so here he is now, standing in a russet sport coat in a long hallway choked with people, nodding and smiling slowly as Mick Jagger—aging but still as lithe and expressive as he has ever been—leans in and whispers something confidentially into his ear. The cameras zoom in and out. Cut to the snack tray. Hugh Hefner and a Playboy Bunny. The members of some rock band we barely remember now. White Snake or Loverboy or Poison.

And over these badly filmed rooms we hear the sound of her vomiting. And then their voices, his and hers:

Are you all right?
Just morning sickness again.
Jeez, I thought it stopped.
Yeah, well me too.
Maybe you should come lie down.
OK.
Hang on. Let me get you a water.
Maybe see if they have a 7 Up downstairs.
A 7 Up?
Yeah, I think that might help.
OK, I'll be back. I'll be right back.
I'll be here.

A waterfall over the pool. Frank in the corner
of some wallpapered room in an ill-fitting plaid
suitcoat. His eyes pass over the room but we are in
the long years before Caitlin—before he knew she
existed at all, her life and his own not yet inter-
twined—and so he cannot find her amidst the
mingling Playboy Bunnies and rock stars. Hefner's
smoking jacket. Oh how he laughs, the smoking
jacket like a silk waterfall hanging limp over his thin
frame. His laughter is the laughter of full red lips
and the pinched flesh of overripe cleavage.

Frank sips a martini awkwardly, nodding as a
woman he will never remember tells him stories he

does not care about.

Can we go now? he says.

He turns to look at you now, right through time and memory and into your eyes.

Can we just go home?

This one was called *For a Short Time Only*, he says, his finger tapping the image. Probably the first big thing I did. I mean, large scale.

Poole glances briefly into the lens, his expression one of surprise.

Read it? Yeah I can read it, I guess. His finger moves to the first line of text, tracing as he reads. It says here, "Frank Poole's work is a representation of suburban America like only 'Frnak' Poole could do." See that? It's misspelled so it says 'Frnak.' Pretty funny. 'Frnak' Poole.

Around him the hotel room is achieving something akin to the disorder of their Iowa home, although in miniature. Frank's disaster of books, notes, maps, and papers has spread out from the corner of the room where he sits now at a small square desk, stacks covering its surface and piled up across the shag-carpeted floor. Caitlin has rented the room across the hall to use as an office. Each of them needs their own space and she has seen it often enough to know that this disaster of material is part of Frank's process, the part that she is witness to and no one else. Some of the materials are those we saw in Iowa—treatises on architecture and design and on suburbia and American life—but the top layer has zeroed in on something else. Heidegger's *Sein und Seit* in its original German. Prior's *Papers on Time and Tense*. Smith's *Language and Time*. Various titles on designing and repairing clocks. Diagrams of gears and springs.

These are scattered around him, although we do not linger on such titles now. Instead, we lean in more closely over his shoulder.

Yeah all right, he says now. Let's see here. His finger continues to rest on the page from which he has been reading, its tip pointing to the text below a color photograph of a collapsing, paint-peeling gray house at the edge of a farm field. He resumes his reading, slowly, carefully: "The fact that most people can't differentiate which building is a Poole sculpture and which is a regular home or business is part of the force of what he does. Poole tests our awareness and our ability to understand what America has become."

He pauses, rubs at his eyes. Sheesh. Just seems like a lot of babble, really. He shakes his head as if to clear it of the idea. Yeah, I think I'm done reading that.

But then Caitlin is here, leaning over his shoulder and continuing with the end of the passage. "Poole tests our awareness," she reads, "and our ability to

understand what America has become. This is true
even of his earliest large-scale projects when he was
in his early twenties, namely *For a Short Time Only*
and *For Sale / Not for Sale*. These are seminal works
because they helped define what Poole was going to
do in the future. Even those pieces were possessed of
a kind of situationalist black comedy that is breath-
takingly simple and yet heartbreaking all at once.
Decay celebrated in one and arrested in the other."

She kisses him on the cheek quickly. See that
wasn't so hard, she says.

Poole shrugs. Decay celebrated, he says. I don't
know about that.

Caitlin has returned to her position on the bed,
one of the few spaces in the room not consumed by
Frank's books and papers. Aren't you gonna tell them
what the house is? she asks.

What?

You heard me.

Yeah, I guess, he mumbles. Then he says: That's
pretty much the house I grew up in.

Pretty much? she says.

Yeah, OK, that's *exactly* the house I grew up in.
A pause and then: Yeah even the caved-in part of
the roof. The whole thing. Just like that. He looks
puzzled for a moment, glances toward where Caitlin

sits looking at her planner and the calendar, and then says, So the idea was to do it from memory but it was also supposed to go the rest of the way super fast. Sort of cave in on itself. Took three weeks. We filled the walls with bread.

He turns the page in the book, apparently a monograph on his own body of work. The next image covers both pages but it is unclear at first what we are looking at, what the photograph is intended to convey. And then we understand. It is a farm field, the same field as in the previous photograph, and the dark swell of earth in the foreground is the last vestige of structure from the crumbling house, now reduced to an unrecognizable heap of damp, decayed muck.

I thought we could make the whole thing turn to mold. You know? So there were like loaves of white bread all packed in the walls. Six hundred loaves of white bread. The whole thing turned to mold in like two weeks. This photo is probably something like two weeks after that. Just a pile of furry ooze.

He stares at the photograph, the look on his face something akin to amazement, whether at the project or at the passage of time or at something else entirely.

Smelled amazing, he says. Like super sweet. But

thick like mushrooms too. Sheriff blocked it all off for like a hundred yards because the city was afraid of getting sued.

Probably doesn't even make sense to anyone now but I was pretty happy with it then.

He smiles.

I was probably something like twenty-two, he says. Barely out of school. I don't even know if I knew what I was doing then. I don't even know if I knew who I was yet.

He ruffles his hand through his hair.

Shit, I'll probably say the same kind of stupid stuff twenty years from now about the thing I'm doing right now.

Let's hope not, Caitlin says from the other room.

Frank does not respond, continuing to stare down into the image. That muddy green field. Bare trees entangled on the blurred horizon. And the small faint rise of what was once a replica of Frank Poole's childhood home. A dark patch of gray moldy earth like the creeping fungus of some horror movie monster.

[4]

Perhaps Frank is not present now. Perhaps there is no interviewer and no film and no web of text to scrim over this illusion. Perhaps there is not even you. Perhaps we are merely listening to her thoughts. The turning light. Perhaps it is the sun. Her eyes are the palest brown. Around the iris, tiny flecks of bright green.

> *We met at a project called* Your New Dream House. *That's right. I was a senior in high school.*
>
> *No, I think he had started doing that before. We all knew who he was. I certainly did. But, you know, he was part of that thing for us. I mean that was the time. We listened to Pavement and we all liked Frank Poole. That was like local hero kind of stuff. We'd see him in town sometimes and everyone would be all like, "Hey, there's Frank Poole." You know. That kind of thing.*
>
> *So, yeah, when he was looking for people to help on* Your New Dream House *I was way into it. Really everyone was. I mean all us art kids. So, yeah, I think he had like thirty or forty people showing up to help but it was like real work, hard work, so lots of them kind of dropped off after a while.*

I guess they all thought that it would be like "hang out with the famous artist guy." And it was like that but it was also super hard, physical labor, all the time, every day. And he'd just keep going. If twenty people were there we'd all be working on it and he'd be working and then if everyone split, he'd just keep on working, like a machine. I mean, physical stuff but also just going through the research like he was a lawyer or something. That's one thing that's still going. I mean, it's like the thing is almost done being built and he's still researching it like he's going to figure out some better way to present the idea or something. Right up until the last day. I mean literally right up until that moment, he's still reading and looking at images and diagramming and stuff.

What? Yeah, I stayed. Of course. I mean, obviously.

Have you seen it? It's kind of messed up now but the idea was that it would be sealed so you couldn't ever go in. You could look in every window and it was all perfect but there was no one home. He even had a glow on the stovetop under a pot full of water that was fake-boiling. Yeah, but no people.

Look, I'm not going to tell you the point but

think about it: a sealed house that looks perfect
and clean and ordered but there's no people who
actually live there and there's no way to actually
get into the building.

It's all a put-on though because it's all fake. He
did something like that too near San Jose with
that Starbucks. I guess people try to go in there
all the time but it's not really Starbucks, you
know. It's another installation. So they try the
door and whatever…it's always locked.

The semiotics is as follows:

A house in ruin. Rain coming down through a hole in the roof and spilling into the living room.

A series of buildings. Empty offices. Anonymous homes.

Street signs. Boardwalk. Main. Martin Luther King Jr. Blvd.

Starbucks. Costco. Wal-Mart. Home Depot. Kroger's. Safeway.

And then we are inside where rows of perfect vegetables in neon colors occupy a produce aisle. Every tomato the same. Every head of lettuce. Every stick of celery.

No people. Not ever. Only structures. Arrangements. Signs.

*Yeah, sure. Everyone loved him. He was Frank
Poole. I mean, what do you want me to say
about it? We were all art nerds and he was Frank
Poole. He had been in* ArtForum *and* The New
York Times *and all of that. He had gotten out
of here and had done exhibits everywhere already
and he didn't seem that much older than us. I
mean, yeah, he's older but he just seemed super
cool then.*

*Me? Who knows. I guess I would have gone to
art school or something. Cranbrook or somewhere
like that. I don't think about it much now. It's
all Frank.*

*Twelve years. We've been married twelve years.
Hard to believe.*

For the briefest moment: a surface of sparkling
blue ice.

Then white light.

Then nothing at all.

SAFE

The landscape of America is rabbitbrush and
bitterbrush and thistle and sage and the thinly
visible roadbed moving between them, Interstate
80's traffic noise fading and that last huddling settle-
ment, Golconda, already a faint collection of slight
sheet metal boxes diminishing in the cold dust that
is your wake. Apart from the roadbed itself, there
is no sign of human life through the windshield.
Instead what comes is only a flat plain flanked by
bare mountain ridges, the peaks of which are named
after soldiers and hot springs and men whose lives
have faded into an endlessness of sagebrush as far as
the eye can see. Black rhyolite and white quartz. The
pale streaks of calcic horizons.

The smoke tail is so faint at first that it seems a
mirage. But if so it is a mirage which does not fade

with your approach but increases, thickening and becoming more broad until you see that it is not smoke at all but the same dust that has marked your path from the moment you turned off the paved road.

The dust is evidence of progress, for now you see that the gap in the wall is almost closed and the roof is more than half-complete, that pillar of wispy dust extending from a vast hole in the metal panels, a hole in the center of the domed roof trusses. And indeed you can see the whole structure of the building now, for it *is* a building, a building of enormous size, covering the entirety of the project, a mile wide and round with a domed roof. You can envision its completion, at least from the outside, can see how it will sit in this desert for all time, like some immense flying saucer come to land in the sage.

Through the gap in the wall—now not much larger than a double-lane of blacktop—appear a maze of arcing roadworks like a labyrinth or mandala roping together the rising squares of two-by-four frames that will, one day soon, achieve the shape and size of residential suburban homes. Now they are only skeletons and even these sometimes disappear entirely, leaving only the bare sandy soil crisscrossed by the indented evidence of heavy equipment and men we can see just a few yards away across the site: tractors and trucks and assembled workers in hard hats, their labor marked by the incessant chirping of huge vehicles reversing over the flattened landscape, by the hiss of hydraulics, by the roar of diesel engines. Pipes for electricity to disappear into the ground. From here you can see the underside of the roof trusses, their lines marked by enormous warehouse lights that hang every few dozen foot in a grid, not yet lit, not able to be lit until the solar panels are put in place along the curved dome of the roof. By then the project will be nearly complete.

Frank and Caitlin stand in the center of that mile-wide circle, on the pale gray concrete disc that forms the center of that center. There are no roof panels above them, the gap there like an enormous skylight, but the winter sun is low, projecting diagonally across the interior of the building, striking the distant framework houses a quarter mile away.

Perhaps the area in which they stand will be a small plaza of some kind when the project is finished, but for now it is only an empty space surrounded by spiraling roads and dirt lots and scaffolded building sites, all of which are, of course, contained by the curved exterior wall and the unfinished warehouse-like enormity of the roof. Before them, the contractor we met earlier holds open the master blueprint of the whole site and the three stare into its whorls and lines. It is not professionally drawn but rather exists as a detailed sketch in Frank's shaky hand. A crop circle to be rendered in concrete and asphalt and lined with finely simulated suburban homes the color of cartoon ghosts.

We did that prototype and it worked great, just like you said.

Yeah I thought so, Frank says.

I was a little surprised, actually.

Were you?

Well, only because I've never done it like that before. These things are usually sort of trial and error.

I wouldn't have asked you to do it if I didn't know it would work, Frank says.

I appreciate that, the contractor says. Kinda like a big Lego set, really?

That was kind of the idea, Frank says, a faint smile pulling at his mouth.

I just hope when it's done it has the effect you're after.

What effect?

I mean, that it looks like you want it to look.

Normally I can judge things off of code but this thing, I don't know. You're gonna have to tell me if it's doing what it's supposed to be doing. I've never done anything like this before.

Is that why it keeps costing more than you told us it would?

What's that?

It's costing more than you bid, isn't it?

Most of that has to do with equipment rentals and materials. Material cost on something like this is what changes. It's a big project.

No kidding.

Is there a problem?

Frank does not look at him, indeed has not made eye contact at all during the exchange, instead casting his gaze out toward the distant wall that rings them a half mile away in all directions.

There's no problem, Mike, Caitlin says in the silence.

The contractor looks at her and then glances to Frank again. OK, then, he says. I'm just, you know, doing the job.

I think we're done for now, Frank says, and without waiting for a response of any kind he swivels in place and moves off in quick stiff steps to the edge of the concrete circle and then into the dirt and dust beyond.

Both the contractor and Caitlin are frozen on the concrete disc, watching him recede in silence.

He doesn't seem real happy, the contractor says after a moment, rolling the blueprint into a tube.

Frank's figure is already small as it moves toward the half-mile radius to the blank gray face of the wall. His stiff gait produces a short tail of moving dust that drifts without direction, fades, and is gone.

He's going to be like that, Caitlin says. He gets pretty worked up when there's a project and this is the biggest project he's ever done. She pauses and then adds, This is the biggest project *anyone's* ever done.

I'm just trying to get the job done, the contractor says.

Just try not to lose your temper with him, all right?

He can be pretty difficult?

Sometimes.

Well, that's something to look forward to.

There is a beat of silence between them.

Thanks for the advice, the contractor says.

Just trying to get it done, Mike, she says.

Me too, he says. Me too.

[2]

This is the wedding photo, she says. We had a bigger one but who knows which box that's in now.

She holds the photograph up to us. It is a faded some with age but we can still recognize them. Here stands Frank looking sheepish and nervous in a 1970s-era powder blue tuxedo. And Caitlin, beaming in her ivory dress. They stand in a field somewhere, in green grass that rises nearly to their knees

This is near Topeka. That's just where we were at the time. Frank was kind of between projects so we just sort of drove around for a while, you know?

She continues to hold the photograph, in silence for a long moment, and then sets it aside and lifts another. This time it is a Polaroid of Frank standing in front of a gas station convenience store, holding a paper bag in one hand, the other signaling a thumbs up.

These are all from that trip, I think. Frank, Frank, Frank. Here's me, sleeping. He likes to take pictures of me sleeping. No, I don't like him to do that. Seems creepy or something. I don't know. Plus you're asleep and then there's this big clicking sound of the camera next to your head. Hard to ignore that, you know?

She continues to sort the photographs. They are strewn across the table, these tiny squares of white-framed time.

Here it is, she says. Here it is.

She slides the photograph forward. Their Iowa home: a plain-looking yellow ranch house on the picket fence-lined court we have already seen, a row of hedges under a broad bay window. Frank stands in front of it in a t-shirt and jeans, a broad smile across his face. In the white strip below the frame is written: August 1999.

So this is the house. We'd been married maybe a little over a year. And he kind of got on this Midwest kick for a while. I mean I was still pretty floored that I was married to Frank Poole, in all honesty. I still sort of looked at him like he was a super-famous guy.

This is in Iowa near Iowa City. He got a job doing some lectures at the university there so we decided we'd buy a house.

Yeah, well, so he didn't really tell me what he was trying to do with it. I mean, I didn't know that everything was for something yet. You know? Well, yeah, I mean like with Frank it's all part of some thing he's working on. Mostly something internal, you know? So it's not always something that'll become a project that other people will be a part of.

He's working stuff out for himself. All the time.

You know, I've been married to him for coming up on twelve years and sometimes I still don't know what he's thinking.

Yeah, so we looked at a bunch of houses. Some of them I really liked. But he really wanted this one. Just a plain, generic ranch house, like out of some weird old subdivision. It was even at the end of a little court and they don't really have too many of those in Iowa City. Or at least they didn't in 1999. Sometimes I think he would've wanted whatever house was there in the court, like that was the important thing. Who knows? Maybe. But he seemed real happy with the house when we got there. He was just about bubbly he was so happy about it. Like it was just the perfect thing, this flat little plain house out there on this dead end with a couple other houses.

She pauses in her monologue, her fingers on the photographs.

Well, I was married to Frank Poole, she says. I was just happy to be a part of what was happening. I didn't know anything. I was nineteen. Maybe not even nineteen yet. I don't know. Him? He's fifteen years older than I am.

She falls silent, but we have not yet finished watching her nor looking at the photographs upon the table. There are so many, but one, in particular, draws the eye. A large white bowl containing what appears to be a dozen or more hand grenades, at the center of which is nestled a bright red fruit, perhaps a pomegranate.

From somewhere in the room: a ringing telephone.

And then her voice again, very close, amused but faltering: Oh god. That.

And her hand, hovering for a moment above the photograph that has drawn our attention, as if she means to remove it from our gaze but has caught herself in the act of doing so. When she does finally draw it from the pile, her actions are slow, embarrassed, perhaps even apologetic. That's from forever ago, she says.

There might be a hint of sadness in her voice. Or perhaps there is always a hint of sadness in her voice, a minor key, a loneliness.

We hold on the photographs. Images that might have been of any young couple on a road trip in the early days of their life together.

From the near distance, the ringing telephone stops. Then Caitlin's voice:

Hello?

Oh hi, Mom.

So we're good then? the contractor says.

Yeah, we're good.

OK, I'm gonna go out to the other side then and make sure the electrical conduit is all ready to go.

Fiber optics too, Frank says.

Yep, I'm on that too.

And in the next moment the contractor is gone, driving away from them in his green golf cart. They are nearly at the wall now, standing with their backs to it, looking toward the center of the project, the line of houses and frames of houses and support beams all appearing, from this angle, to be in a particular order, their lines receding into the distance like orchard rows backlit by the sunlight slanting through the huge gap in the center of the roof. The contractor's golf cart recedes toward that light and then turns out of their view. Where they stand is in the shadow that the roof makes, the lights in place but no power yet. A colorless quiet darkness along the edges.

Hey you, she says.

Hey you back.

She comes to him and puts her arms around his puffy jacket and they embrace there. He kisses the top of her head, glances up at the wall, the roof thirty feet above them. The low sides of the dome.

A few road signs visible around them. 12:15 PM COURT. 7:45 PM ROAD. 5:30 AM WAY.

It's coming together, she says.

Sure is.

It was just a bunch of paper last year.

I was there, he says.

She smiles.

The street. The signs. The gray wall.

She pulls her head up and looks at him. You get any sleep last night? she asks.

A little. He stares down at her, his own face in profile. You know how it is.

I do, she says. She smiles at him, faint and pale.

He had looked at maps of mineral flatlands and the contour lines of ridges and hills and mountains. What remains on the page now are two people set in profile in the shadowlands beside an enormous gray wall.

You doing OK? he asks her.

Yeah OK.

Not feeling sick anymore?

Less now. Internet says it ends around week twelve.

What week is this?

Twelve.

Ah.

She pauses. Then says, It's gonna be amazing.

Are we still talking about the same thing?

I think so.

Good. He looks around himself at the scene as if searching for something to affix his gaze upon. Then he says: I don't know what else to do.

It's coming along, she says.

Frank glances up at you briefly, his eyes flickering across the lens, across the screen, a gesture so fast you do not know if you have seen it at all.

Neither of them speak for a long moment and yet you remain with them, holding this shot, without edit, without movement, the camera simply rolling through the silence.

Then Caitlin, her voice a quiet murmur: What are you thinking about?

My dad, he says.

She nods, as if she knew all along that this would be his answer. You're not going to be like he was, she says. You know that? You're not going to be like that.

How do you know?

Because I know you, Frank Poole.

He gently pulls her head against his chest, his hand on his hair. I don't want to mess it up, he says.

Is that really what you're worried about?

Mostly, he says.

She looks at him, just briefly. We have seen the look before and we recognize, now, its impatience. You can still do your work, she says after a moment.

Not like now.

Well, she says. She seems to hold her breath for a moment, her shoulders high and sharp. Then she tips into him, into his shoulder, settling against him for a time.

As if in response to some cue, they both turn and begin to walk toward the street and away from us. His arm is around her shoulders. Hers around his waist. A thumb tucked into a belt loop.

We'll have to make some sacrifices, she says, her voice close.

A beat of silence.

Frank? she says.

And his voice: I heard you.

The pole at the intersection offers no street sign to give a location or a time.

[4]

A blizzard of digital lines. Then a gas station convenience store.

Frank turns toward us, beckoning to follow him through the glass door and into the fluorescent-lit interior, Caitlin's voice continuing all the while, disembodied now:

> *I don't have any photos of that. I don't think*
> *Frank does either. I've never seen any*

He is talking, although we cannot hear his words. Not now. Instead, we only see his hands moving in the air, his eyes where they dart toward us and then away again, as if embarrassed to be listened to so closely, to be followed into this space. He leads us down one of the aisles. Chips and Corn Nuts. Beef jerky in strips. Midway down the aisle he stops and looks up toward the fluorescent lights, looks up and says nothing, only staring as if he can see through the building, through the light tubes and metal and ceiling tiles and into the sunlit sky beyond.

And Caitlin:

> *Well, that's a good question. No, he hasn't been*
> *back there in a long time. Maybe a decade and*

then he went back once more when he was doing that piece, The Pantry. *No, that's where he did the convenience store in that apartment. He didn't tell you? No, it's exactly the store where his mom's house used to be. He had a surveyor figure it out. The vantage point from the pantry door in that apartment is where the roof had caved in. I mean exactly, to the inch, you'd be standing right under it. He spent a ton of time figuring that out.*

There's a film of it somewhere. One of the times he went back there that 60 Minutes *show came and interviewed him in the convenience store. You should find it and put that in the film.*

And now we can hear the soundtrack to the footage we are actually watching. It crossfades with Caitlin's voice, the room-sound of the recorded interview falling away, replaced by the hum of the convenience store. The commentator's voice—it sounds like Ed Bradley and probably is—is close and confidential, asking him how it feels to be back here, back in the place where his mother's home once stood.

And Frank takes a long moment before answering, continuing to stare up into the lights until, abruptly and without warning, he turns his gaze to look directly into the camera lens, directly into your eyes as you read these words, his mouth curling into a grin. It feels great, he says. It just feels great.

Ed Bradley asks him to explain why he seems so happy when the site of the home he grew up in is now a gas station convenience store.

Well, look around, Frank says. It's perfect now. It's all clean and in rows and organized. It's just a perfect space.

And now we zoom in, Frank's eyes brown and luminous and his face filled with a sense of joy that we have not yet seen, perhaps a joy that he has not felt since that moment in 2002 when he stood at the location of the house where he grew up and found that it had become a gas station convenience store.

Safe, he says. That's what I'd call it. Safe.

STILL LIVES

[1]

Tractors along the street. The workmen in
their hardhats. The house before them appears in
cross-section and we can see, for the first time, the
elements that are complete and the elements that are
not. Everything within view of a window is perfect.
Even the furniture is in place within—white sofa
and white walls and white television with its screen
tuned to static. But there is an area of the stairwell
that is simply absent because it cannot be seen
from the outside and no one, of course, will ever be
allowed within once it is complete. The men who
stand inside the opening now ready themselves with
nail guns to receive the wall.

And then it comes. The workmen press forward
and the wall section comes up all at once, like an
enormous slice of white bread, textured with stucco,

already finished, even on the inside surface, to match the interior paint. It lifts like some barn-raising in an Amish town and closes upon the gap and the sound within is not unlike gunfire. That thick slice of white bread fitting into its position in some huge edible dollhouse.

Behind us, walking now into view, are more work-men. The foreman is waving them on, gesturing to the group and then to the doorless opening into the house. Their movements are slow, at too low a speed, and their hands swing through the air as if pendulum weights at the nether end of a huge wire. Some carry tools. One a bucket of paint; you already know the color. Black men and white and Hispanic and Native American.

They disappear one at a time through the door. The pendulum. The great swing of rotation. Then briefly at the windows: passing shapes that are there but for an instant and then dissolve out of our view.

[2]

You ever think about doing something like yoga? the doctor says. The image on the screen is of static, as if someone could simply move the rabbit ears and the whole thing would come into focus.

On the hospital bed, her brow furrows and she half-smiles in surprise. Yoga? she says. No, why?

Well, your blood pressure is a bit high, the doctor says. And you said you've been spotting. That's of some concern. He moves the wand across her belly. My patients tell me that yoga helps them get rid of their tension.

You do it?

Not for me, he says. I'm a runner. That's how I get rid of my stress. I guess the question is: Are you doing something to deal with all this stress?

I don't know.

Well, let's be thinking about that, he says. Here's what we're looking for.

In the wave of static is a shape. A circle and a line. What am I looking at here? she says.

Well, that's the baby's head there. Its skull. That's an arm and that bumpy line there, that's the baby's spine. You see it, Dad?

Frank looks at the doctor briefly, perhaps surprised to be addressed in this way. Then he peers past his wife at the screen and nods. He is not touching her now. He is only standing beside the bed, staring at the monitor. A skittering, grainy image. That's the baby, he says.

Yes, that's the baby. The doctor busies himself measuring on the screen, using the joystick and keyboard as if playing a video game.

Can you tell if it's a boy or a girl? Caitlin asks.

Well, sometimes, but this one's at a pretty hard angle. If we can get the little one to move… The doctor presses hard with his wand, Caitlin's small belly pushing in on one side.

Don't do that, Frank says.

It's all right, Caitlin says. He knows what he's doing, Frank.

It's all right, the doctor says. So, Frank, your project will be done in a month?

What?

Your project. It's going to be all done in a month?

Yeah, I think, Frank says. His eyes do not leave the screen. I mean we hope so.

Might be a little longer than that, she says. These things run over schedule.

The doctor is talking to Caitlin now. Well, maybe that'll solve the whole problem, he says. With your blood pressure, I mean.

Maybe.

Yeah, this baby doesn't want to move for me. The doctor has continued to digitally mark and remark objects on the screen and after a time he says, Doesn't look like we can really get an ID on the gender.

Too bad, she says.

Sometimes it happens that way. If you really want to find out we can work harder at it.

No, it's OK, she says, I don't mind the suspense. That OK with you, Frank?

He shrugs. Says nothing.

We said probably eighteen weeks and I think that's about right. So we'll officially call it eighteen weeks. That makes your due date April 29. How does that sound?

Sounds like spring, she says.

He wipes at her belly with a towel and then hands her a clean one and she does the same, leaning up and rubbing off the warm slippery goop he has used to lubricate the wand against her skin. The shape of her pregnancy has been mostly hidden by her thick winter clothes but it is bare and apparent now, the curve of the coming child. When she is done wiping her skin clean, she pulls her shirt down and buttons her jeans.

A small rectangle of paper has been printed by the machine and the doctor hands her that sheet now. A grainy image of their child's head, arm, and spine awash in a black sea of static. There's the little guy or gal now, he says, smiling. Pale face and white hair. I think I'll want to see you in about a month just to make sure everything's going OK.

All right, she says again. Thanks for seeing me. She has swiveled to the edge of the reclining chair and stands now. Frank jolts out of whatever thoughts he has been having and holds her arm as she rises to her feet.

That's what I get paid for, the doctor says.

He turns to leave the room but then stops and faces her again. It's gonna be great, he says. Takes some getting used to but you'll be good parents. You'll see. It all comes natural.

Caitlin's hand curls into Frank's, the two of them in the room, staring out at the doctor, his shape an illuminated silhouette in the doorway.

Good luck with the big project, the doctor says.

Thanks, Caitlin answers.

Frank continues to stare toward the light of the doorway long after the doctor has disappeared.

This is its grammar. Like the measure, the
sentences unscroll in straight lines across a grid that
is apparent only when the map is in your hands.
Comma the corners, the bends. Make them points
of watching from one phrase or clause to the next,
the flow of words coming over the asphalt in a thick
torrent. Your suburb or purlieu or selvage or skirt.
Your juncture or pass. Your point in time or stall or
centre. To locate yourself upon such a flow is to attri-
bute that location to a grammar of logic and place.
A fixedness, not just upon a geography but upon a
time. She should know this already. Or at least we
should think so. After all, is she not the one who
keeps the whole works moving? Even now she kneels
in the dirt, drawing geometries upon a sheet of graph
paper with a pencil stub. Tick tick tick and the whole
thing effluxes to the next moment. Even now, every
word you read is time you will never recall from the
funnel. And so elabe. And so lapse. And so the run
and the roll and the sleve. The whole of it flits away.
Everything growing in the containers into which they
are born. Telophase. Anaphase. Metaphase. Prophase.
The gaps into which the cell cleaves into a zygote.
Two cells. Then the morula's spherical cells align. The
blastocyst. The embryo. The fetus.

The color is white. There is no denying. He knew that before he started, well before he even had the idea of the thing in itself. *Das Ding an sich.* That was part of it, but time itself is white for him. The blank page. There could be historical arguments made, of course—or sociological or ethnological—but he does not think in such terms. Time the animal to be caged. As if such a thing were possible. And yet he would try. Fathers and sons. The man and the boy the man once was and whatever comes after. A boy. A girl. Of course they do not know.

Come up now, above the whole of it, not yet complete but taking shape each day, a thing squatting in the desert with nothing around it at all, the only access road being that which the construction team has built and which will disappear once the project is complete. Make no mistake: This is his Levittown, his Naperville, his Bayville and Dunewood. The place he did not grow up in, the place he could not even have imagined in that rotting house with its caved-in roof. Strike that from your mind now. Let it be erased. Instead, marvel at how perfect this new place could be, will be, the whole thing arrayed as a precise circle in a wasteland with only that dim strip of temporary road connecting it. The last part of the project will be to wipe that clean. Not even the desert, then. Only the steel wall. No door or window.

No exit or entrance. And no time. One day soon.

[4]

Again the home movie. The scratched film. How
it leaps off the sprockets, clacks and breaks apart
and comes back together again. The man laughs in
silence. The man breaks into pieces. The man laughs
again.

A scattering of black scratches.

And white white light.

You should wear that hardhat I gave you, the
contractor says.

Yeah I know, Frank says.

This is twelve noon through…down there, let's
see…three fifteen. Right? I think that's right.

They walk along a row of white houses assembled
based on Frank's design, this area closer to completion than the area in which Caitlin continues to do
her measuring. From the outside they look like any
suburban homes. Ranch style. Perhaps from the
earlier years of suburbia but nonetheless of a design
we recognize. White roof tiles. White stucco walls.
White doors. Through the windows, we can see
their white interiors. White walls. White sofas. The
televisions are not yet powered up but they will be
tuned to white static.

The support beams holding the roof trusses in
place have been wrapped in white plastic casts from
a real tree, each the same tree replicated over and
over again, the branches of which lay in heaps beside
them, yet to be raised, yet to be assembled. It is like
a landscape constructed entirely of powder.

It's four per hour, Frank says. That end should be
through three thirty p.m.

You're right, you're right, the contractor says.

You should know that.

I'm not sure it much matters since it's all the same house.

It matters.

How so?

It matters because it matters. This end is two thirty p.m. That end is three thirty p.m. That's what they're called.

OK, the contractor says. Whatever you say. Two thirty. Three thirty. Got it.

Don't patronize me, Frank says. His tone is cold and flat.

I'm just trying to do the job you hired me to do, the contractor says.

Is that what you're trying to do?

The contractor is quiet for a moment, his jaw set tight in the cold winter air. Maybe have Caitlin come see me later, he says quietly.

What for?

Look, Frank, I'm doing my best here but you're getting all bent out of shape about stuff that doesn't affect what I do here at all. You could call this house LaVerne and that one Shirley and what difference would it make to me? I'm still assembling the same house in the same place.

It matters because it matters. Things have names.

Things are specific. That's the point.

Well, like I said, Frank: Whatever you say.

You just don't get it, Frank says quietly.

And I don't have to, the contractor says. I just do what's on the paper.

Goddammit, Frank says, his voice rising now. That's what I'm talking about. The specifics are what the whole thing is about. It doesn't work if it's just generic. That's not the goddamned point.

We can call things whatever you want to call them, the contractor says.

Just stop, Frank says.

The contractor spreads out his arms and lets them fall, a gesture of surrender. Then he turns and takes a few steps away before swiveling back toward Frank once more. Buddy, he says, your wife said you were going to be difficult to work with but you really take the cake. I've got my people here working overtime building houses no one is ever going to live in and you show up every day to bitch about every goddamn thing.

Frank stands looking at him, blinking slowly.

Now you don't have anything to say?

There is a tractor backing up across the building site before them now, its shrill hard beeping and the roar of its diesel engine washing over whatever the contractor says. In the next moment he turns and crosses the street, disappearing around one of the nearly complete buildings.

Frank stands in the vacancy, on that empty street, the sound of tractors echoing out across the desert. That single row of white houses with their white roofs and white trees and white lawns. The cracked earth skittering out in all directions. In the long distance, Caitlin's figure is a dark shape moving amongst houses so white that they seem to waver as if part of a mirage.

Frank looks to you just for a moment, then tilts his head back. His eyes are damp but perhaps it is from the cold.

[6]

The room dark. A faint cut of blue light through the curtains.

He clicks on the light. He is already sitting up. She stirs slowly beside him.

I can't sleep, he says quietly.

OK, she says. Her voice is murky, head still on the pillow, half-turned toward him, squinting.

I'm going to watch the feeds or something.

All right. She turns her head back to the pillow and closes her eyes.

Frank reaches off the edge of the bed and brings the laptop up from the floor and sits tapping at the keys.

After a few moments she half-turns again. How long you gonna do that? she says.

I don't know.

She exhales, drops her head to the pillow for a moment and then raises it again. I'm gonna go sleep in the office, she says.

You are?

Yeah, just come get me when you're ready to go back to sleep.

Maybe I should go do this in the office.

All your stuff is in here, she says. Just come get me when you're done. An edge in her exhausted voice.

All right, he says.

He leans down and kisses her briefly. Then she rises, padding to the door in her bare feet, dodging books and papers all the while. She lifts the room's key card from atop the dresser by the door. Don't forget to come get me, she says.

I won't.

They exchange goodnights and she opens the door and is gone. Frank does not look up again from the laptop. His face is blue in the screen glow.

The images are from the project site, live video feeds. There will be nearly one hundred different angles when all the cameras are in place but now there are only thirteen. Rows of unfinished white houses and rolls of material that will be, one day soon, white lawns.

He moves through the angles again and again and again. Far into the night. So far into the night.

TIME

[1]

Night in the desert.

The signs are in place. Every one. Green with reflective white letters pasted to flat metal plates. They glow in the floodlights.

If you were to follow them out in any direction, you would find time moving in fifteen minute increments on a twelve hour clock moving from a.m. to p.m. the farther away one gets from the center. But there are other times as well. Or rather, not times, but ideas about time. At a given crossroads, you might find yourself at Just In Time. Or nearing No Time Like the Present. We turn from 8:00 a.m. Court onto Lunch Time and then find ourselves rounding onto Killing Time. Good Old Times, yes, but there is no Saving Time nor is there a Stitch In

Time. Frank Poole would tell you that he does not believe in such things, such abstractions. He would tell you that you can only kill time, not save it. He would tell you that allowing for any such possibility is foolish and wrong.

Some insects, night-winged, like stars across the white flow of the streets.

Then a sound: a woman's voice. Not old. Not yet old. Never to become old. But weary nonetheless.

> *Frankie? Frankie? You hear me? Bring your momma a Co-Cola, all right?*

You could place a huge set of clock hands across the whole round suburb; those hands would follow the signs around and around but what time would it tell? What is at the corner of Lunch Time and 6:00 p.m? What kind of time is that?

Such thoughts are complicated by the circular plaza that lies in the center of the project. It is a flat concrete disc now and in the center of that center: a concrete tube sunk into the earth, six feet in diameter and extending thirty feet below the surface, descending into black shadow. This is where the clockworks will be assembled, a design based upon Frank's ideas and then clarified through a collaboration with a horological engineer and a San Francisco firm specializing in the fabrication of precise machines. Some of the papers you have seen in Frank's research piles have been the hand-scrawled workings of this clock, the pendulum and weights of which will drop down into the concrete tube, the opening to be fixed, in the end, with a bare clock face without hands, the face itself turning slowly, the weights continuing to drive the pendulum, the square mile of solar panels that already cover most of the roof providing enough extra energy to keep the whole thing operating long after Frank and Caitlin and you and I have all gone into our separate and timeless graves. One day soon it will be clean and white and smooth, moved by a great pendulum that will tick the escapement gear forward despite the fact that there will be no hands. Not saving. Not killing. As good as a blank face. And yet not blank. One day soon a numberless clock face spinning at the center of a white space comprised of homes without residents, streets without cars, every structure perfect in its simplicity, identical to the first, identical to the last.

Frankie? I'm still waiting on that Co-Cola now.

[2]

Once more.

Laughing. Coming to pieces as the film springs loose of its sprockets and goes dancing at the edges of light. The laughing again.

He leers out at the camera from darkness, his face a blur, his hands pawing the air. He is the father, not the son. The father. Do you understand me? The father.

Remember this:

A scattering of black scratches.

And this:

White white light.

[3]

And his voice, yelling out through time, through all the years, out past death and into the decay of the house. Water pouring down the walls, splashing against the warped floor, the soggy rotting carpet, the furniture they did not move: a soaked and stained and mold-covered sofa, a few battered wooden chairs, a collapsed bookshelf heaving with swollen newspapers the individual pages of which have welded together into a slurry that is both solid and liquid.

And his voice, his yelling voice, comes from somewhere deeper in the house or perhaps from another scene entirely: Goddamn you. Just let a man enjoy his goddamn night off, goddammit.

And there is water. So much water pouring down the walls, pouring across the floor in streams now, in rivers, spraying through the cracked glass of the windows. The sofa adrift. The chairs toppling into the swirl. The current coming up around the room. Sofa. Newspaper. Broken glass. Wood. Plaster. All of them on rafts of death. All of them into the current.

[4]

And black in that water. Black.

> *Frankie, are you going to bring me that*
> *Co-Cola or aren't you?*
> *Yes, Mom.*
> *Well, I've been calling you about five times*
> *now.*
> *I know.*

You would reach into that current to grab hold of
them—a shirt, a hank of hair, perhaps a thin pale
wrist—but there is nothing to hold in that swirl,
nothing but water, loose bits of trash, scraps of sodden
newsprint. Your hand would curl around such things
nonetheless. Hoping one might transubstantiate into
flesh. Into your heart. Into time itself.

> *Baby, you know he doesn't mean it. You hear*
> *me? He doesn't mean it.*
> *I know.*
> *Do you?*
> *Yes, I know.*

Black water in your hands. It is your heart. It is
your blood.

OK then. Now come here and watch some TV with your mamma.

All right. Scoot over.

A black street ending in a T and lined with white houses, only some of which are complete. Others are two-by-four frames. Partway down the street lies a stack of walls.

Then we are looking in through a window at a living room with all white furniture: sofa, chair, television tuned to pure white light. White curtains hang at either side of a more distant window open on a backyard of white grass surrounded by a white fence.

The next is simply a flat space of dirt. Some white fencing behind it. A stack of building materials.

> *I used to dream of it when I was a kid. You know? Just a perfect space. All clean and white. Everything in rows and organized and empty. It was like a kind of heaven. And even as a kid I knew it was impossible. Because the house we were living in was just coming apart all around us. And I used to think it was just the house itself. The actual physical space. But it's not that. It's time.*
>
> *Think about it like this: If you could just stop a moment—a single moment—wouldn't you do it? Wouldn't you pick the best day of your life and*

just hold it there?

So it's the perfect space. The most perfect space that I could imagine. Pure empty perfection. And in the center of it, to represent some notion of what that perfection is really about. Right? You can't stop it but what if you could strip it away so that it no longer has any actual meaning? What if it's no longer important? What if it no longer exists in the way we think about it?

I don't know how long that thing will run but really it doesn't matter to me if the clock stops. I mean the effect of it is still identical to itself if the thing doesn't even run. That might even be better, really. A clock without hands that ran for a while and then stopped—all in the middle of a perfectly round totally white and self-similar housing tract. Because it's not about the suburbs, it's about time. That's the thing that keeps coming up for me, over and over again. Preserving that moment of perfection. That's why McDonald's and Starbucks and all that too. It's like that stuff's perfect for a moment, but it's the moment before anyone cooks a hamburger or turns on the espresso machine. After that it's just a fast food place. But there's a moment just before, when everything is assembled and clean and shining. There's just nothing better than that moment. It's perfect. It really is. Nothing can go wrong. Nothing can get fucked up or hurt or anything. It's just perfect for that one instant before anything happens. And then time. And everything to come after.

There is no motion, no movement at all. The houses in various states of construction. The roads empty. Stacks of building material. From somewhere just off camera, a crow flutters into the frame, hops briefly upon the fresh asphalt, and then flaps away.

GRENADES

[1]

There is a haze of snow in the parking lot now, although the late morning sun's heat has already turned it to slush, runnels of meltwater slipping down into the broken gutters that line the street. The culverts hiss with its current.

The Mercury's great broad hood rocks as the car pulls into the lot from the street. It has become filthy from days of rain and snow and the dust and dirt of the desert wind. Even so, the sun winks against its grime-smeared windshield as it turns into a vacant space in the lot.

The door squeaks on its hinges and a moment later she steps out onto the wet asphalt. She does not look at us. She does not look at anything.

He wasn't there, she says.

Now we see her eyes, if only for a moment.

Ringed in red. Her cheeks wet with tears.

He wasn't there, she says again. When she moves away we do not follow but watch her, receding, pulling out of focus as she reaches the glass doors of the casino, the reflection of the parking lot shifting momentarily across her disappearing shape. In that reflection is all of Nevada. In that reflection is you, reading these words.

[2]

If furniture continues to stand amidst the papers
and books there is no trace of it now. The whole
of the room has become a kind of research sculpture comprised of the materials of Frank Poole's
particular intellectual mania: papers, photographs,
books, diagrams, charts, drawings and scrawled
notes. Architecture and design. Leonardo and
Hopper and Thiebaud. Philosophy and art and the
labyrinth of time

The adjacent room—the room Caitlin uses as
her office—is nearly bare. On the desk, a few thin
stacks of papers flank a black laptop, the screen
displaying a swirl of rainbow colors. The familiar
calendar of illuminated religious manuscripts is
tacked to the wall near the door.

She is seated on the bed. We have not seen her
smoke before but she is smoking now, taking
an occasional puff as she speaks into the phone,
breathing it out into the stale air of the hotel room.
An ashtray rests on the leather-bound planner
and she taps the cigarette against its edge with a
frequency that is well beyond need.

I don't know, she says. I just don't know.

Puffs and taps. Her eyes are bloodshot.
Occasionally a tear slides down her face, her words
punctuated by sniffling.

The police? I don't know. Probably. I'll drive
around some more first and see if I can find him.

Yeah well, what do you want me to say? He's
my husband. No, I'm not playing the martyr. Are
you gonna do this now? Because if you are I'm just
gonna hang up.

She waits for her mother's response, puffing on
the cigarette, its tip glowing brightly in the dim

hotel room.

Yeah, OK. OK. You're right.

Hey, look, if anyone from the media calls—I mean at all—you can't say anything. I'm serious. Because the funding is super tight right now and I don't know how we're gonna finish it as it is. I didn't tell you this yet but the contractor quit this morning. Just didn't show up so none of his crew was there. We got there and it was just silent and when I got back to the room I called him and he said he quit

He said he just wouldn't let people treat him like that anymore. Frank, I mean. I didn't even really know he was having a problem with Frank until he called. I guess they got into an argument or something when we were out there a couple of days ago.

I know, I know it's his fault, mom. I know. You don't have to keep telling me that.

She sits listening now and as she listens tears return to her eyes and pool there. The cigarette clenched between her fingers shakes, the phone held away from her mouth.

When she speaks again, her voice is steady and calm.

You know I'm not going to do that.

There is a long moment of silence. She takes another drag on her cigarette.

No, I'm not smoking. I'm pregnant. I can't smoke.

Her hands tremble.

I love you too.

I will.

I gotta go.

She stands for a moment, the phone returned to its cradle. Then she is running.

She very nearly does not make the toilet, bursting through the door and flipping the lid up just as the retching begins, her hair a tangle across her face, hands trying to hold it back but also gripping the edges of the bowl. Face down. Face down in the acrid smell of that vomit water.

[4]

Her voice is quiet and mostly without emotion, perhaps even flippant, as if she is speaking from earlier time, some days or weeks or even months before.

> *No, I didn't end up going to college at all. It's like if you want to write songs you don't marry Paul McCartney. You marry—I don't know—someone who's not Paul McCartney. Bob Jones.*
>
> *Why would I regret it?*

She sits by the window in the bare room. Then unfolds her legs and stands. Then sits again, smoking. What light slashes through the curtain burns with the setting sun. Outside, the street moves on below. The line of fast food restaurants. Cars circling the edge of the wet parking lot. The grime-covered Mercury filthy in its row.

The cigarette's thin ribbon of smoke curls upon the air. A white line. A cloud.

Finally she stands again, moving to the door and slipping into her coat again and stepping outside into the hall.

5

We follow her now as she crosses the casino floor, through those banks of slot machines, through the laughing, drinking figures. She looks for him, as she has already done several times, her walk a kind of circuit now, her eyes casting back and forth along the aisles of machines.

At the front desk she rings the metal bell and then stands waiting, picking at a cuticle with her fingernails.

The man who appears wears a blue Western-style shirt, its silver buttons shining in the dull ringing air. Hello again, he says, a thin smile upon his lips.

Any news?

Afraid not.

All right, she says.

I'm sure he'll turn up, he says. He's probably just out having a time.

She does not nod, only holds his gaze for a moment and then turns and walks away, not toward the stairwell but out through the glass doors and into the cold chill of the night, crossing the parking lot to the sidewalk, cars sliding past her on the roadway.

He'll be in a bar, she says. I know it.

She does not look at you but only continues

forward and when she sees the flashing neon sign of Nick's, its green shamrock flickering beside it, she angles to the door and pulls it open and steps inside.

6

We might think to follow her, but when the door opens it is upon a photograph projected on a wavering screen, the frame centering on a white glass bowl arranged upon a surface that we cannot see in any detail, the bowl seeming to float in some atmosphere comprised solely of cloth.

Of course, our eyes do not focus on the cloth but rather on what the bowl contains: some number of hand grenades, amidst which sits a single red pomegranate, its color so bright, so fresh, even with the faintly washed-out quality of the slide, that its effect is to heighten the harsh knobbled surface of the grenades: ominous, deadly, green. One thinks of salting a watermelon. How such an act brings the sweet to the fore.

When the slide moves forward—and it is indeed a slide—we can hear the hum and mechanical shuffle of the projector, one slide raising up in the plastic wheel, the wheel itself clicking forward, the next slide dropping into its slot, the process clear and bright and perfect even through the cheap plastic, the burning bulb.

Like the previous image, this one is a carefully photographed art piece and it is again comprised of a bowl of hand grenades. This time, though, there is no pomegranate; instead one of the grenades has been partially peeled, its knobbled surface split and curling back to reveal the surface of a blood orange within. The other grenades in the bowl: Who knows if they are fruit or real grenades? They seem no different from the partially peeled grenade. They seem no different from grenades.

And again, her voice, faintly animated by emotion, coming across the miles and across time:

> *My dad thought those were funny. Well, the peeled grenade he did. The other one he just said it looked nice.*
>
> *Politics, sure. What can I say? I was in high school when I made them. You know—young and idealistic, for sure. Seems silly and innocent now. Grenades and pomegranates. Making a statement of some kind.*
>
> *Frank? I don't really know. He's never really said anything about them.*

There are others too:

A photograph of a field of daisies, each yellow disc replaced by the black and white shape of a skull, rendered with such clarity that it seems as if the stamen themselves have morphed to make the shape. Across the bottom of the image is scribbled a single word: *realpolitik*.

Then another. It is a wider shot of the daisies, this one showing the wooden box they have been arranged in, the bare metal stems pressed into a foam block, the painted sky on a sheet just behind. She stands against that painted sky like a giant, leaning down toward them, mugging for the camera, sixteen or seventeen and smiling like we have never seen her smile, perhaps like she has never smiled since, a girl, a young woman, on the brink of her life. Who could say what might come after? Would it not be as glorious?

[7]

The field is green. So bright and so powerful that it seems as if it could not possibly be real. And yet there it is, flanked by sculptures and partially shadowed by trees. It appears a palace garden of some kind, albeit one marked by a distinctly modernist design, for the sculptures are objects of clean lines and balance, the building in the background something between Bauhaus and ancient Greece: clean pillars fronting a glass wall.

> *Cranbrook.*
> *It's funny—it still looks amazing to me, even now.*

A red metal sculpture balancing in a green field. The shadow it casts is a series of thin black lines upon the grass.

> *Well, I was going to go. That was the dream. I was just nuts for all those guys for a while: Charles Eames, Donald Lipski. Oh, Duane Hanson, I still love his stuff. Frank does too. They're in the same line.*
> *No, they've never met. They'd probably just stare at each other anyway.*

A series of glass squares arrayed in a vast three dimensional circle, suspended in space. Clear. Magnificent.

Other sculptures too. Metal shapes balanced in thin vertical air. A red disc cut against a golden, geodesic dome.

> *Well, I didn't think so at first because I didn't think we'd be able to afford it but my mom and dad, they were always super supportive of whatever I wanted to do. Dad even told me he'd take out the equity in the house to pay for it if that's what I wanted.*
>
> *Anyway, as it turned out they offered me a scholarship so that wasn't even an issue. Funny how you worry about stuff and sometimes it just works itself out. And then, you know, I didn't end up going anyway.*

[8]

And then we are in the car with her, the cigarette held between her teeth, the traffic lights changing to green. Fast food restaurants. Small casinos. Night traffic. She turns the wheel. Turns again. The lights spin slowly, leaving long tracers, as if the camera's exposure is set too long, the lens allowing too much light into the aperture so that nothing fades, each image piled upon the last, time itself a long snake pulling forward into a future that has already arrived.

> *When? Just before Frank came on the scene.*
> *After that I just did something else.*
> *Cranbook? No, never. I guess we just never*
> *made it over there. I don't know why.*
> *Frank's a busy guy.*

The red point of the cigarette has become a jagged shape in her hands.

IT'S WHAT'S FOR DINNER

[1]

The voice is Frank's:

My dad? He was a drinker, for sure.
You want me to say more? Like what?

Who can say what is in the mind of a man other than by looking at the things he has made? A series of buildings representing a relentless exploration of a single topic. And they write about it as if they know, but who can say if the topic they have fixed upon is the correct one? A man's mind ranging over a landscape only he can see and no one to step behind and stare through his eyes at the world but himself and so stare he does, into streets and buildings, through lit walkways and dark doorways, and across cities and towns and vacancies, and even into the eyes of the woman he loves. But what does he see there but himself, in all those landscapes, and in the eyes of his wife. Everything a mirror. And so everything the same.

Well, he couldn't really hold down a job. So he would leave town for like three or four months at a time. Then he would come back and it would be pretty great for a while. Honestly. I mean he was my dad, you know. I was a little kid. And it was great when he came home.

Yeah, he'd have like presents from wherever he'd been. Nothing big but like stuff you could get at a truck stop gift store. So like I had a Indian spear from when he had gone down to Oklahoma for a job. I probably still have that somewhere out in a box.

Electrical contracting, mostly. But he'd take anything at a building site. He was pretty handy. That's why it was so ironic, you know, that the house fell apart.

The family has gathered around a long formal table. They make some small talk, their words indistinct. The father asks the daughter how school was. He asks for the peas. The white bowl arrives in his hand. The mother wears a brightly colored sundress. The son is perhaps ten and wears a tiny tie that makes him uncomfortable. The daughter is the eldest at fourteen and wears a dress not unlike her mother's. They talk, this family, in a kind of halting, hushed formality, as if posing for the camera, and perhaps that is exactly what they are doing. They each seem hesitant to actually eat, as if doing so would be rude to the viewer or to you reading these words. The mother smiles. She might be forty. Perhaps slightly younger. These children the only children she will ever have. There is sadness in her face, in her eyes, a sadness that is all the decisions she has ever made, each easier than the alternative and each pressing her into a tighter corner. Her husband is a kind man. Her children love her, and yet here she is, at this absurd table. Had she described it, it would look like everything she has ever wanted. And yet now that her life has arrived, it seems a vacancy from which there is no escape.

She looks at you. Can you feel her gaze? The light in her eyes is upon you and you drift past her, over the table and across her gaze and beyond, for you are not here for her, you are here for something else and already it stands before you: the bright light, the glass-blocked doorway through which exists a world different from this one and yet completely the same.

Through that doorway at the far end of the dining room is a convenience store. Rows of brightly lit freezers containing soda. Aisles of candy and beef jerky and, at the periphery as we pass over the table and beyond the father and to the glass itself, a sales counter with a cash register, a half-full bottle of soda behind, a rack of cigarettes, a wall of hard liquor in tiny bottles. And beside it, on the inside of the swung-open door, a silver plaque that reads:

The Pantry
Frank Poole
Mixed multimedia installation, 2000

Her face, once more, standing in the kitchen. The table filled with the dirty plates and serving bowls and silverware. The family gone somewhere. Gone to watch television, perhaps, and she remaining behind, standing stock-still, the table stretching out behind her, her face smiling and then relaxing. She says something you cannot hear. A question, perhaps. But then her face is emotionless. The smile gone. All expression gone. And she is simply empty. Vacant. Numb.

[3]

*Look, it was that he'd be all right for a while
and then one night he'd just be silent, like, at
the dinner table and then he'd snap at my mom
about something. I don't know what. Like she'd
ask him if he could fix a light that had gone out
or do something around the house and he'd flip.
Just like a light switch or something. One time
he threw his dinner plate and it literally cracked
across my head. You can still see the scar there.
See it?*

*Another time he got so mad he knocked the
whole table over.*

*I'd just run. Sometimes I'd go into my room.
Other times I'd run outside. There was a little
stand of cottonwoods by a creek about a quarter
mile away and sometimes I'd just run out there
and wait until it got too cold. Then I'd sneak
back in through my bedroom window.*

*No, I was like nine or ten then. Yeah, I guess.
Pretty young.*

But then we are already gone, outside now, drifting along some suburban street in the night. Light
posts passing. An old neighborhood with big trees

overarching the road. A car passes slowly, as if watching to find out what we have done, where we are going, where we have come from.

The house we turn toward is lit by a number of footlights which shine upward upon its white clapboard siding and colonial revival architecture. Two thin columns flank its small, covered doorway, the door itself—painted a deep red—topped by a swan-neck pediment above which flies a cast-iron eagle in bas relief.

We are midway across the lawn when that door swings inward to reveal a balding middle-aged man who swivels aside as we move up the brick steps and through the doorway. As we enter, we catch a single glimpse of a woman—his wife, we might assume—standing at his shoulder. She gestures upstairs and we follow that motion, rising up the tan, carpeted stairwell and into a tan, carpeted hallway where two children sit in their pajamas, playing with plastic trains which they grab as they run out of view. But we are already past them, moving to the end of the hall where there is, once more, a glassed-in doorway, beyond which is a kitchen in full blazing daylight, a roast on the center island, sunlight cascading impossibly through the half-open mini-blinds, a pair of oven mitts resting, one atop the other, next to the roast. One can almost smell the cooked meat, its sweetness, its willingness to be consumed.

We have seen this kitchen before, have stood inside its golden sunlight. We can almost see her at the little rolltop desk against the wall adjacent to the sliding glass door. We can almost see her sealed within.

The plaque again, this time:

> *It's What's for Dinner*
> **Frank Poole**
> **Mixed multimedia installation, 2001**

When I first met Caitlin I was drinking a lot. Did she tell you that already?

It's a little hard to talk about. Yeah, it makes me want to have a drink. Sure. Just makes me, I don't know, uneasy. I guess that's the word.

And then another. This the last. A night-smeared New York City street. Uptown. A suited doorman pulls open a glass door. A marbled lobby within. An elevator. A man and woman are with us —he in a suit, she in an evening gown—but when the elevator doors open again we leave them behind, floating down a red carpeted hallway where widely spaced doors close off the opulence within. But then, at the far end of the hall, a single door swings inward and we continue to move, passing through it into a two-story apartment with floor to ceiling windows looking out on an amazing cityscape where the Statue of Liberty blazes. But we are not here to see such a symbol. Instead, we swivel around, passing the figure of a man in a suit, who watches us blankly as we drift, as if free of gravity, up the stairs and into a book-lined study, its dark wood panels making the whole of the room appear darker than it actually is.

Here, a man sits at a black desk, writing on a legal pad, and he glances up as we approach, acknowledges us with a terse nod, and then reaches behind to pull a book halfway from the shelf. Upon this motion, the bookshelf swivels inward, the whole of it hinged as a massive door, and immediately from within comes that now-familiar blaze of light.

What lay within, seemingly impossible in its size and scale, is an entire McDonald's restaurant nestled into the secreted confines of this apparently massive apartment with its bookcase doorway. Of course, we can only see it from this one vantage point as, like all of Poole's installations, this one is blocked off by a glass wall. But here it is: the curved plastic benches in bright red and yellow, the gray table tops, all of it in rows upon a checkerboard floor. The lit menu with its photographs of menu items. Beyond the menu and the registers stand the shining steel of the kitchen, the deep fryers, the table for preparing food where we can see, if we crane our necks just so, the rows of tomatoes and lettuce, the burgers coming off the fryer, the drink machine ready to pour. It might be identical to any McDonalds in the city but if so it is clean and perfect and ready as if never used. Frozen there. Time arrested.

The plaque revealed by the open book-door is silver and reads:

Dinner Time
Frank Poole
Mixed multimedia installation, 2002

When we turn back into the room, the man is holding out a McDonald's cheeseburger to us. He smiles broadly. He has a sense of humor, this apparently wealthy benefactor of art, this man who, we assume, allowed or encouraged Frank Poole to install this replica McDonalds in his expensive New York City apartment. He doubles over with laugher as he holds the cheeseburger and we watch him there, his silence in that dark, book-lined room, the flat white florescent light of the McDonald's installation cracking his face into planes of light and dark, his face, his body, the walls, the desk, the books, and, somewhere, the Statue of Liberty. All of it broken to pieces.

[5]

We are with Caitlin again. She has returned to the casino, her shoulders dusted with snow, shoes soaked through. In her walk, we can see evidence of her pregnancy, her gait heavy, shifting. The slot machines are bright but we cannot hear them, for instead there is Frank's voice:

It's funny because she asked me just the other day if I thought about drinking at all. I guess she's worried because there's a bar downstairs in the hotel. But we've stayed in lots of hotels that had bars. You know?

The elevator then. She presses the button. The doors close. What rising there is comes in utter stillness. As if there is no rising at all.

I told her that I don't think about it at all. It's true. Mostly. I mean, of course, I'm thinking about it now because that's what we're talking about. And sometimes when I can't sleep. I used to take a shot of gin if I couldn't sleep. That used to help. But yeah I don't do that anymore.

Well, I mostly just get up and read or something. Back home I'd just go out to the front

room and keep working. Eat some ice cream or
a Hot Pocket or something. Here at the hotel? I
don't know. I try to read. Look at photographs.
Definitely harder to power down.

I should probably buy some ice cream
somewhere.

He laughs at the end. His voice a dry leaf. A sheet
of paper. A fluttering rag.

But now Caitlin has come out of the elevator and
has rounded the corner and there he is, seated on the
carpet, his body slumped against the door.

Frank? she calls, her voice a brief sound like
a querulous bird. Then she calls again, moving
forward with speed now, her footfalls heavy against
the carpeted floor. Frank?

He does not look up at her until she is there by
his side, kneeling, her hands upon his face. He
is soaking wet, dripping, the carpet a damp pool
around him. I forgot my key, he says, his voice a
thin whisper.

When she grabs him, the action is so surprising,
so visceral, that the camera itself seems to jolt with
the shock of it, her small hands on each side of his
face, grasping at him, his cheeks, his temples. Frank's
eyes are wide, staring back her.

You can't do this, she says, her voice trembling with a barely suppressed rage. You can't fucking do this.

I'm sorry, he says.

You don't…

I'm sorry, Cait, he says again.

Shut up, shut up, shut up, she says, the rhythm of it like a hammer striking a nail over and over again.

His eyes struggle to focus even as his face shakes from cold, the skin pale and pink through the unshaven stubble of his beard.

You have to be here, Frank, she says. That's the only thing you have to do. You have to be here.

I am here.

No, you're not, she says, shaking her head slowly, tears standing in her eyes. She drops her hands from him.

I'm here now, he says.

That's not good enough. She hovers there before him for a long, trembling moment as his clothes drip silently onto the carpet. Then she reaches up to touch his face, one palm on a cheek, then the other. You're freezing, she says.

I'm sorry, he whispers.

Don't say that anymore.

I'm sorry, Caity.

Come on, she says.

And somehow, using all of her strength, she manages to get him to his feet, to swipe the keycard through its slot, to open the door, and to pull him, stumbling and half-unconscious, through the door.

INTERIOR / EXTERIOR

[1]

We have nearly forgotten about the park but we are here again, returned to its green sward, its picnic tables, the suburban homes that line the nearby street. It feels like dusk, or close to dusk, the sun beginning its slow movement that will result, within the next few minutes, in that brief flashing moment that filmmakers and photographers call the magic hour, no hour but a scant ten or fifteen minutes in which everything within the lens is blessed with a golden contrast and a sense of warm suffusion that is impossible, at all other times in the day, to achieve.

We do not have the golden hour yet, but we can feel it coming.

A flock of starlings on the wind, then settling in a tree, then rising in a brief cloud and settling once more. Their voices: a sharp stabbing wave.

Frank and Caitlin say nothing. The ice cream containers are empty and they hold them and stare out, both, into the distance somewhere, Caitlin moving just slightly as she sits there, her hands shifting position, her head tilting. Frank, of course, is still and quiet as a stone.

We circle them, these two, and as we pass, their twin gazes follow us. In hers: a sadness and sense of unrest. And in his: a bottomless emptiness.

How you feeling?
Terrible.
You all right?
I don't think so.
What do you want to do, Frank?
I want to be someone else.

The lights click on. Fully furnished interiors now covered in cobwebs and dust. The sofa unused. The television clicking on and the stations changing slowly but no one watching. Then, as if in response, sprinklers in the backyard burst into hissing sound to wet an overgrown lawn. Someone has spray-painted part of a word across the dust-obscured sliding glass door:

FUCKHEA

A few beer cans on the concrete patio.

Upstairs the bed is made. Light comes slantwise through the dirty windows. A layer of black dust on the sill and, buzzing lethargically, a dying housefly. Down the hall: a bedroom for children. Bunkbeds. Everything tidy and arranged.

The adjacent homes perfect and clean and occupied, but this one house: eddied with dust and advertising circulars, weeds sprung forth from concrete seams.

A man walks back and forth, pushing a lawn-mower across one of the nearby perfect lawns.

Then we see this man as if in interview, although his voice is muted. Static. The scrape and flutter of percussion. His t-shirt ringed with sweat. Short hair as freshly cut as his lawn. He gestures toward the empty house with a clear sense of exasperation, irritation, perhaps even anger. He mimes knocking it down or knocking someone out. Perhaps both.

[3]

They sit together in the casino restaurant in
Winnemucca again. A few scattered individuals
in the background, each eating lunch or breakfast
depending on the flow of their day. The ongoing
and faintly muffled sound of the slot machines, their
vaguely musical digital beepings drifting amongst the
diners like the ever-present scent of cigarette smoke.

You want to find a meeting? she asks him. She
does not look up, staring instead into her eggs and
wheat toast.

No, I don't want to do that.

Maybe you should.

I don't think so.

What do you want to do then?

I want to finish the project. Then I want to
go home. He clips off his last words and coughs
roughly into his napkin, the sound thick and hacking and wet.

You can't drink, Frank.

I know that.

You can't do that again.

I know that too. I didn't do it on purpose.

She looks up at him now. His face is wet with
tears but his voice is steady and calm. I need to
know where you were, she says.

I wasn't anywhere. At a bar down the street. At another bar. I can't remember much after that. Does it make any difference?

I went to every bar I could find.

That's where I was.

She shakes her head slowly. Let's go home, Frank. Let's just go home.

I have to finish it, he says. He looks across the table to her now. I have to finish it first. I have to. He breaks into a hacking cough now, takes a long moment regaining his breath.

I think you need to go see a doctor.

No, I'm all right, he says.

Jesus, Frank.

Just let me finish it. Then we can talk about what's next. It's the one thing I can do.

What does that mean?

I just need to finish it.

No you don't.

He does not answer now.

Look at me, Frank, she says. Look at me.

His eyes come up now, red and filled with sorrow.

You're not like your dad, she says.

What if I am?

You're not. He was a drunk asshole. You're Frank Poole.

So what?

So you're going to take care of this. You're going to work on it and you're going to take care of it and you're going to be here for your child and for me. That's so what.

He only stares at her, stares into the emptiness of her face.

You need to take care of this, Frank. I'm serious.

I will, he says. But I have to finish the project. I have to.

She shakes her head.

I have to, Cait. Nothing works if I don't.

Dammit, Frank, she begins, but he has broken into the coughing again. This time it doubles him over at the table, the sound harsh and sharp and he is gasping for air, his sunken eyes going gray and sweat coming in slick droplets across his forehead.

She is already rounding the table to come to his side.

[4]

Black screen.

There was this one day. It was Christmas or close to Christmas. And it was my mom and me in that house. We were in the room where we had the television set up. I don't know where my dad was or where he had been or anything but I remember there was a knock at the door, which was weird anyway because no one ever knocked at the door, and I ran to open it and there he was—my dad—with a big Christmas tree. It was amazing. I just felt…I don't know how to describe it…just pure joy, I guess is what it was. Pure joy.

We set up the tree and he even had lights and some ornaments and everything. And he was there for Christmas and had gotten me a truck that I really liked. You know, like a Tonka truck. It was yellow and had a dump truck bed. Super cool. I kinda wish I still had it actually.

Yeah, I remember thinking that this was like a real Christmas. Like the kind of thing you might see on television. You know? And I was also thinking that it wasn't going to last. I mean I knew that already about him. I was probably eight or nine that year.

*Yeah, well, he left altogether when I was ten
and then showed up for about six months when I
was a teenager and after that I didn't see him at
all until the funeral.*

*When was that? 1998. Liver failure. Right
before I met Caitlin. I mean right before—like
a month before or something like that. I already
had* Your New Dream House *all set up and she
was one of those teenagers from the high school
that came to help out. I probably should have
canceled the whole thing but if I had I wouldn't
have met her.*

From the black comes the project. We see it in
fast forward, in timelapse, a single day as home
after home is snapped together as if pieces of an
enormous puzzle. White Astroturf lawns unrolled
and tacked into place. Bleached trees concealing
the support towers. One after another. Everything
in place, the light flat and even across the expanse.
No days or nights in which to mark the passage
of hours. No sun but that which Frank Poole has
placed above them.

GOLD

[1]

Here, drink this, she says. She tips the straw against his mouth and he drinks weakly from it. A single swallow. Then his head drops back to the pillow. His face damp with sweat, hair plastered to his forehead. She puts her hand there. His eyes are closed.

You're burning up, she says.

I feel terrible.

You look terrible.

His teeth chatter. He has the blankets pulled up around his neck and he screws himself down into them now.

Here's the thermometer, she says.

He opens his mouth and she places the instrument between his lips and he lies there with half of it protruding, eyes closed, head tilted sideways against the pillow.

She sets the 7 Up can on the nightstand, dodging his books and papers all the while. A cut of light extends from the bathroom's half-open door but otherwise the room is in shadow. She sits on the edge of the bed and opens her planner and then lifts the phone and types in a number.

Hi, she says, this is Caitlin Poole. Yeah, that's right. No, I'm doing fine. But, uh, my husband Frank has a bad flu or something. I was wondering if you could recommend a doctor who might be able to come over here to the hotel. Yeah, I know but he's really sick. Way sicker than I've ever seen him. Yeah, hang on.

She leans over the bed and says, Open, and extracts the thermometer and then sits looking at it. It says a hundred and four, she says into the phone. Maybe closer to a hundred and five. That's pretty high, isn't it?

OK, OK, I'll do that right now.

She clicks the phone off. Shit, she says. Then: Frank? We have to go to the hospital. Right now. Come on, Frank.

She moves to him and puts her arms around his shoulders and tries to pull him forward. His head is loose, as if it has worked free of his body. His breath comes as a heavy scratching in the air.

Come on, Frank, she says. You have to help me.

She lays him back down and scrambles across to the phone again, the stacks of books and papers scattering in her wake, punching the zero and then saying into the receiver, I need to get my husband to the hospital. Can someone help me? Please? Can you send someone up to help me?

[2]

The hallway blurs. His feet stumble against the carpet and then simply drag against its surface. The two men carry him by the shoulders. She runs before them down the hall. Out of focus. The hall tipping. The world tipping over and away.

[3]

The blur and then the blur again.

White fish in dark water.

Then her hazel eyes.

Then charts of subdivisions, one after another, huge and intricately formed shapes like cross-sections of lung tissue. We expect it to shift once more but our focus holds now. Cul-de-sacs within cul-de-sacs stretching off the edges of the map in all directions. Russian nesting dolls. Chinese puzzle boxes. Invisible cities made real. This is the map of the gravesites of America. The death of time.

And Caitlin's voice:

> *We did a road trip, I guess it was two years ago now, because he wanted to see the old projects again. I don't really know why. It might have been when* ArtForum *did that long piece on him. So we went to look at most of them. I mean, the ones that are still there, because the earlier ones were designed to decay quickly. They were like hyper-time pieces. That's what* ArtForum *called them. That's a pretty good way to put it really.*
>
> *We started with* This Too Can Be Yours *up in South Fork. Right? Yeah, it's there. So perfect.*

Just like the other houses, only it was earlier, so like those other houses were still being built and Frank's was done and it was all on timers and everything. So it was like people were living there but there was never anyone home, you know? Like it was some ghost family or something.

As she speaks: the empty rooms again. We have seen this before, this space. A dead fly on a window-sill. The lights flicking on and off. The television changing channels.

Well, yeah, it was kind of disturbing. For both of us, but I think it really hit Frank kind of hard. I mean, he gave that piece in trust to the university there and they kind of ignored it. I mean something like that has a lot of maintenance, you know? You've got to make sure the stuff still works at least. I mean, there's like graffiti across the back of the building now. Right in the suburbs there, in that court in South Fork. That kind of thing.

Yeah, of course, I did. I called and read them the riot act on the phone. But what are you gonna do?

Well, yeah, so part of the project was that it

was sealed. I think that was the first one that
he did like that. Sealed because he didn't want
anyone in there messing it up. Yeah because it
was supposed to be analogous to the museum
pieces he did in Cincinnati. The same kind of
thing. With everything sealed off and frozen.
And that one, you know, he called it This Too
Can Be Yours. *This perfect little world held in*
a kind of freeze. Right? But then it was kind of
falling apart anyway

Well, yeah, he didn't say anything but you
know he was upset by it. I can tell, you know?

Here stands the neighbor again. This time he is
facing the front of the empty house, looking up at it,
his gaze as implacable as the building he faces. The
garden hose he holds is the bright green of all garden
hoses, the arc of water clear and cool and bright as it
splashes against the concrete sidewalk.

Yeah, well, the point was that they were sealed
so I'm sure his head went right to all the other
ones. Sure, there's Tall Grande Venti *and* Park
Place *and* Brownstone *and* Your Credit Is
Good As Gold. *Yeah, some of those are busi-*
nesses and some are apartments and stuff. Oh,

*and the ones that are like sealed rooms inside
other people's homes. There are like a half-dozen
of those. Yeah, they're all titled works.*

No, that's Tall Grande Venti. *It's like a free-
standing Starbucks. He did another Starbucks
that's more like a diorama project. That's up
in Albany in some fancy house. But* TGV *is a
whole storefront in a strip mall. That's my favor-
ite because people are yanking on the door all the
time and wondering why it's not open. Hilarious.
There's even a drive-thru and a voice asks you
for your order. Well, it's my voice actually. And so
people talk and talk and talk and then they drive
up to the window and there's just no one in there.*

*No, he really loves those spaces. He really does.
People call it all kinds of things. A critique of
capitalism. Stuff like that. It drives him crazy.
He just wants to preserve the space. That's all he
cares about, really. He picks things like Starbucks
and McDonalds because they're really beautiful
physical spaces. That's what he thinks.*

The neighbor stares at you. Will you answer his
gaze? Will you tell him what he wants to hear? He
breaks into pieces as the film goes off the sprockets.
Then he is laughing. In pieces again. Laughing.

[4]

He opens his eyes against the darkness and there she is, asleep in a chair.

Hey, he says. His voice is rough sand. Hey.

She stirs. A hospital blanket around her. Light blue. The window behind her is rendered in pinstripes of hot white light, cutting the black shadows of the blinds.

Hey, he says again.

She looks out at him through her hair. Sees him awake. Leans forward. Hey, she says.

Can you get me a drink?

She pulls a pink plastic cup off a rolling tray and leans in toward his face, tipping the straw into his mouth. He sucks at it, swallowing, and then leans back against the pillow again.

He looks down at his arm. I have an IV? he says.

Fluids, mostly, she says. And antibiotics.

Wow. I don't think I've ever had an IV. Kinda grosses me out a little. Can I have another drink?

She again tips the straw to his lips.

Are we home? he says when he has once again leaned his head back against the pillow.

We're in Winnemucca. At the hospital.

Right, he says. OK. Winnemucca.

You're pretty sick. Pneumonia and everything.

Still hurts to breathe, he says.

Yeah, it's gonna take a while, she says. She stares at him and then reaches out to cup his face between her hands. You scared me, she says.

I think I scared myself.

Don't do that.

I'll try not to.

She kisses him on the forehead then and he lays his head back on the pillow.

I'm super tired, he says.

You should sleep.

How long have I been here?

Since yesterday.

Wow.

Yeah.

Should I ask about the project?

Right now you need to sleep.

He looks unconvinced but he closes his eyes anyway and does not open them again.

She drops back into the chair, the blanket down around her waist now, her belly a hard round shape there. Her eyes are dark with exhaustion. The IV drips in silence. Various pieces of hospital equipment beeping and chattering all around her.

DISSOLVE TO:

ONE DAY SOON

1

Workmen spool the Christmas lights and place them in clean new cardboard boxes, one team moving along the high front of the building with two tall ladders, a second team down by the big gate that opens upon the street. One of the workmen, high up along the edge of the roof, leans one shoulder against the building's lit sign: Sage Valley Recovery. It is this workman that calls down to Frank: Hey, Franco. Congratulations.

Frank looks up at him and waves. Thanks, Dan, he says.

He stands next to the bench by the concrete roundabout and then sits, a tan suitcase at his side. He is, as always, bundled in the tattered down jacket and the familiar sock hat is held now between his knees. A few orderlies and doctors come and go.

Most greet him and offer their congratulations and he answers each of them by name.

There is a clarity in his eyes, one that we might have seen only in the beginning, way back at the public park in Iowa when he and Caitlin ate their ice cream together, before the project, before any of this.

When she arrives, it is to pull the white Mercury into the roundabout and draw that vast car to a stop.

He is already on his feet, a wide grin across his face. There she is, he says.

She is out of the car. Her pregnancy is easily visible now, a swelling shape partially hidden by her coat.

They embrace there by the car. He kisses her. They kiss each other.

You did it, she says.

I did. Thirty-five days.

I'm proud of you, she says.

I'm glad.

This seems pretty big, he says. His hands are on her belly now.

Twenty-six weeks.

Is it always weeks?

That's what my book says. She looks up at him. I missed you, she says.

I missed you too. I'm sorry, Cait. I'm really really sorry.

She looks at him, his hands still on her belly, holding it as if it were a ball. Her eyes well with tears but she is working hard to keep them under control. You ready to go? she says.

This is what I'm supposed to do. Apologize, I mean. It's called "making amends."

You've already done that.

Have I?

She nods.

There's a lot more I need to do.

Good, she says.

They stand together shyly. Then she says, I've got something to show you.

What is it?

You'll see.

Is it bad?

No, it's not bad.

Is it good?

You have to wait, Frank. She smiles at him, faintly, and then says, Come on, and he nods and opens the door for her and she slides behind the wheel. The white Mercury with its Iowa license plates. The suitcase in the backseat. He is beside her on the wide bench of the front seat, his head already looking out the window.

Where are we going? he says.

You have to wait and see.

The car moves forward, the wide white hood gliding out through the gate and into the road. A flurry of brief, fleeting snow in the sage country beyond. Distantly, the lights of Reno, tilting off to their left and then behind them as they rise onto the interstate and move east, deeper into the yellow desert, the road that leads to Winnemucca and Battle Mountain and Elko. The road that, eventually, will lead them home.

No way, he says.
Way.

But let us see it first from the air, for now the desert ridges are like so many white blankets laid out with their velvet creases and folds and between them, in the great snow-covered plain they shelter from the wind, that great mile-wide disc sits in the desert with one metal door swung open and a blazing strip of light arrowing out from that aperture into the thin wrinkles of snow. We have seen it on paper—seen it in glances and in pieces—but as we pass through that opening and into the lit interior, we see that it is complete now, complete at long last. The effect is breathtaking. So many homes—a hundred or more—all of which lie in white as if the whole of it were sculpted in plaster or cut from clean white pages. Only the streets themselves offer contrast, for they are black asphalt, tracing a maze of circles through those pale constructs, the cul-de-sacs, strips of white grass to mimic public spaces, white plastic trees with white plastic leaves, and, of course, in the center, that concrete disc around which the whole thing seems to rotate.

Wow, he says.

He stands at last in the truth of his creation, his back to the doorway, the interior opening into a perfection of filled white emptiness. All those white homes in rows. No people but themselves. No crime. No alcohol. No pain. Only silence.

Even their breath is white steam in the air.

Here it is, she says.

You did it, he says.

So did you.

The video too?

They're all in place and they all work.

Jeez, Cait. I don't know what to say.

How about thank you.

How about I love you.

That works too, she says.

I want to see the whole thing.

I know you do, she says, but hang on a minute.

What for?

It's a surprise.

Another one?

She walks back out the door, from this side of the wall a black rectangle with a few faint flakes of snow blowing through it. The sound of the car's trunk closing. When she returns she holds a crumpled paper bag in her hand.

What's that?

Ice cream from Bobtail.

No way.

Way. They FedExed it. Merry late Christmas.

What flavor?

Lime with chocolate chips.

No way.

Way.

She is at his side now and he puts his jacketed arm around her and her arm around him and they walk, these two, the paper bag rocking slowly in her grasp.

Everything still and silent around them. Even their voices sucked away from them. Empty houses. Empty streets. White lawns. White white light filling the frozen air.

Neither of them speaks a word until they are nearly to the center of the project, that wide disc that marks its exact midpoint and where they will find a clock face embedded into the concrete, its hours marked out with black dashes but without numerals or clock hands to indicate the hour. Its ticking is a soft rhythm from somewhere beneath the earth.

Does that mean you're going to stay? he says then.

What do you mean?

With me.

She looks up at him now, surprise playing across her face.

They have stepped up onto the concrete disc now and move to its center and stand side-by-side looking down at the clock face and then peering around them. From here the design is easy to ascertain: all those white houses extending out like the spokes of a wheel.

It's really beautiful, Frank, she tells him.

He nods.

You want some ice cream?

Do I ever, he says.

[4]

Ice in the living room. Ice in the kitchen.

A metal bucket, its water frozen into a solid block. Within: a white fish, motionless, suspended. A pale hand rubs powdery crystals from its surface.

Hoarfrost on the broken window glass. The sofa has burst into a jagged explosion of white ice. And of the broken ceiling with its rain: that too has solidified into a collection of rough white diamonds. The carpet visible only through a top layer of clear meltwater ice like the bottom of some frozen-over lake.

We cross the plastic barrier from one side of the house to another, from the broken space where the frozen waterfall sparkles in winter sunlight, and into that part of the house where Frank and his mother lived when he was a child. The television set is still here. His mother's recliner, thinly coated with frost. Seated at a card table, amidst the ice and in a faint glow of refracted blue sunlight, sits Frank Poole. We watch him for a long time. His stillness. His white breath in the air. The windows around him crazed with frost.

When his voice comes it is from somewhere else, where he sits with Caitlin by his side, perhaps in the warmth and security of their Iowa home. A year or more into the future. Where time continues to roll forward. Where you sit reading these last words.

> *Frank Poole. My name is Frank Poole.*
> *Did you get what you needed?*
> *I don't know. It's your thing.*
> *Do I want to say anything? About what? OK, yeah. Well, we named her Grace. Yeah she's great. Healthy.*
> *No, I don't want her in this. You can put all the rest of it in but not her.*
> *What's next? Man, I don't know. I've got a lot of ideas. But right now I've got two hundred ninety-eight days sober. So that's what I'm working on.*

Frank? Caitlin's voice comes.

Yeah? he says. His breath is steam there in the frozen room. His face expressionless. As in a dream, caught up in the crystalline luminescence all around him.

What are you thinking about?

Nothing, he says. His breath shines: white white white in the room.

Frank? Caitlin says.

Yeah? he says.

You done with your ice cream?

A long pause. Then: Yeah, I'm done.

He remains that way for a long time, sitting in that frozen room, the room of his childhood, of his memories, unmoving. But then he turns, so slowly, shifts his head until he is looking at you, directly into your eyes, across time and geography, across these false black letters upon this frozen page.

He is in light. Almost a halo. Almost. And his face: see as it breaks into a smile.

Out of the white come the photographs. We have
seen them before and we do not linger on them
now:

1961. The station wagon pulling the boat. The
family that stands before it.

The bicycles and children of Roseville, Minnesota,
1955.

The brochure of Levittown, Pennsylvania home
styles, circa 1957.

That unknown anonymous 1950s living room,
the family posed and unposed. Her newspaper:
the *Herald Tribune*. Blue birds. Blue leaves. Blue
branches.

But now we are in the other images, the ones
Frank has prepared for us and which Caitlin has
completed for him. We see them one after another,
in increasing speed: streets of white houses, white
rooms, white light filtering through white leaves,
everything the same, quiet, perfect, again and again
and again.

And finally, out of that same bleached colorless-
ness come Frank and Caitlin Poole. They stand
before the steel door in the snow, their hands form-
ing a V between them, both staring into the blazing
white light that emanates from within, the white

Mercury behind them idling softly, its black tailpipe sending a long rope of steam into the air.

When he presses the door closed it merges with the curve of the wall so that it appears only as another steel panel there, indistinguishable from any other, the whole thing an undifferentiated curvature of metal pushing away from them in a great arc across the desert. The only thing to mark the immense structure is a small panel, one familiar to us from the others we have seen in Frank Poole's installations, a panel only a few inches wide and bolted to the side of the wall:

One Day Soon Time Will Have
No Place Left to Hide
Frank Poole
Mixed multimedia installation, 2012

The two figures that stand before it are in darkness now, the Mercury continuing to idle behind them and a few faint dry flakes of snow drifting down upon their heads. We watch as their bodies tilt into one another, as his arm comes across her shoulders, as her head tips into his neck. For a moment the image clatters up against itself, the figures breaking into doubles of themselves, the sprocket holes visible for an instant before the whole thing locks back together again. But now they are gone and it is only the wall and the snow and the white face of the desert stretching across a map of America that is as blank and featureless as a page.

We hold upon that vast landscape, hold for so long that it seems as if the image has become a still. Then comes a flicker, an image so fast and so bright that you wonder if you have seen it at all. And yet you know you have for it burns in your memory of that blank sagebrush landscape: a brief, flashing image of a bowl of hand grenades amongst which nestles a single, bright red pomegranate.

When we fade at last, we

FADE TO WHITE

ACKNOWLEDGMENTS

Thanks to Lydia Netzer for offering honest assessment, good questions, and excellent feedback. Eleanor Jackson continues to be my champion, protector, and friend—a thousand thanks. Gratitude to my 11th-hour copyeditors: Chorel Centers and Josh Lacy; and thank you Don Reid for emergency help with the fade to black. And especially to Deena Drewis, head honcho of all things Nouvella: The world is made better for the work that you do.

Dolores Hayden's work, especially her *A Field Guide to Sprawl* (with beautifully disturbing aerial photographs by Jim Wolk), has been particularly useful. I should also note that Scott Hicks's excellent *GLASS: A Portrait of Philip in Twelve Parts* appeared on PBS when I was midway through drafting this novella. It helped me imagine what *One Day Soon* might actually look like as a film and helped me clarify the language of both documentary biography and editing (via the fine editing work of Stephen Jess). I also owe a debt to the kinoromans of Ingmar Bergman and Andrei Tarkovsky, which gave me the central idea of how to approach this subject on paper. I owe a further debt to two short novels by Don DeLillo—*Point Omega* and *The Body Artist*—both of which offered a tonal resonance right when I needed it. I am also indebted to photographer and friend Jess Newham for introducing me to the New Topographics photographers, without whose work none of this would have occurred to me at all.

Thanks also to my father, Gary Kiefer, who was kind enough to join me for a research trip deep into Northern Nevada and to my wife, Macie, who provided the time.

Last, my profound thanks to Johnny and Caitlin Gutenberger for much too much and for nothing at all. They can currently be found at www.ilovetwosheds.com.